Family Rules

Family Rules

A Novel

VINCENT TUCKWOOD

FAMILY RULES

A Novel

2nd Edition published by:

View Beyond LLC
PO Box 1096
222 Boston Post Road
Waterford
CT 06385-9998
USA

ISBN-13: 978-1468081718
ISBN-10: 1468081713

For Sybil, Jack, Elise and Kyra
I love you very, very much

Chapter 1: Another Anywhere

Where to start, where to start, where to start?

Hmmm...

Well, I guess the start was being born in the UK. I was...

No wait... That's not right.

You don't want to know about that. You want to know how I ended up here, on this couch, talking to you.

This exposé. This kiss and tell. This redemption, this catharsis. Salvation?

You want to know about Bella.

You want to know how it all happened, right?

Right?

So, let's start with what's important, the only thing you need to know.

I have stared into the dark, black eye of oblivion and found comfort.

You know what that's like.

You know what it's like to stare into emptiness, to see yourself reflected there, to place yourself on the other side, to invent yourself in a world that doesn't really exist.

You know what it's like to be a figment of someone else's imagination.

You know that.

And, if the truth be told, we all know that – even if we don't admit it to ourselves.

We are all stories.

And I think to understand it, *all* of it, you have to understand that first and foremost – it really is where it starts and, I guess, where it ends, with me telling you all about it.

I think you'll understand, I really think you will, but it's probably going to get messy before I'm done. It doesn't really make sense to me, not all of it.

It's a story.

We are all stories.

Me. You. The you I see and the you everyone else sees. Friends. Teachers. Family.

All of them stories.

Especially family.

My family. The biggest story of all.

* * *

You know some of it, of course. But let me fill in some of the gaps.

It doesn't really make sense unless you understand.

These things, they... They fill the void.

Chapter 2: Descent

Kurt Cobain.

He shot himself.

I know why.

At least I think I do.

Empty. Running on empty.

Everything he had to give and he couldn't make any of it make sense. The adoration, his art, that tortured soul, Courtney Love, none of it satisfied him. Meaningless.

People wanted to blame the drugs, obviously. Heroin does that, you see; there's nothing except the addiction. Nothing.

Even his daughter... Even she couldn't provide a reason to believe that anything was actually worth something. Or so it seems.

I only realised all this afterwards; when I woke up.

* * *

It lasted for about two years.

Lost days and weeks of chasing and chasing. Never quite present but never fully lost.

Twenty years old and I was already bored with my habit.

It hadn't really worked.

I was still empty.

I found myself in mirrors.

And couldn't ignore the guy who stared back at me.

Me.

This life I'd created.

Bored of it.

Tired of it.

Keen to do something else.

*   *   *

You know about the money, of course. How could you not?

My family was rich.

Which would have been great if it hadn't been for the fact that my wealth didn't actually belong to me. On paper, I was pretty close to making the creeps who win *Who Wants to be a Millionaire?* look like street cleaners. But at that time, in reality, I couldn't even have bought them a cup of coffee.

If only I'd spoken to my parents since I turned fifteen, I might have had some chance of laying claim to the bullion and rocks that had been salted away on my behalf. I mean *really* talked to them, of course.

And being real wasn't something I...

I walked out of the apartment when I was nineteen, fully intending never to come back again.

Another step into oblivion.

Nineteen. On the streets of New York city. Parents comfy and warm on the Upper East side, me dodging from flea-pit to doorway to shelter and hoping to score.

I don't know if they even noticed I'd gone.

I doubt it.

I got threatened at knife-point one night, one guy holding my arms from behind while the other pulled a switchblade back and forth across my adam's apple. Just the tip of the blade, just enough to leave a red mark there that felt a little like shaving rash the next morning.

Someone walked past the alleyway while this was happening and yelled. Knife-boy and his pal ran for it, leaving me wondering just what it was they'd actually wanted to steal from me – they hadn't had chance to say. Not that I had much, about three bucks and a handful of loose change.

The guy who shouted didn't hang around, just grabbed his girlfriend and disappeared down the street.

The attack was enough to bring me home; hoping that there would be a welcome scene waiting for me there. Good or bad, it didn't matter, just that there be a welcome scene. I'd been gone for a month; surely they'd have missed me?

But there wasn't.

They were out for the evening. At separate parties.

So I sat on my own and ate ice cream at the kitchen table.

Once or twice I thought about heading to my room to get high but, to be honest, the reunion was going to be difficult enough.

Besides, I didn't want to give them the satisfaction.

* * *

By the time I was ready to sleep, they still hadn't come home. Probably getting screwed senseless wherever they were. Almost definitely not with each other; I would have staked my three bucks on it.

So I went to bed. Left the door to my room wide open. Left the bedside light on.

They both came home that night.

Slept at home.

In the same bed as each other.

Snoring when I got up to go to the bathroom.

Gone from the apartment by the time I got out of bed the next day.

Not a word.

My bedside light was still on.

No note.

The bedroom door still open.

No reunion.

I wasn't too surprised, why should they have changed the habits of a lifetime in a month.

I ate some ice cream, went back to my room and got high.

After I'd closed the door.

Chapter 3:
Leverage

They're Brits.

He's in management consultancy – uses the word *leverage* in what feels like every sentence – and she...

What *does* my mother do?

It's not earning money, that's for sure. She comes from money, lots of it. Born into expectations of elegance and achievement.

Different generation.

Different class.

At eighteen, she would have been at Swiss finishing school, comparing the bank balance that put her there with that of her school-friends, the trust fund in waiting, wondering which prince she might marry, planning her society debut, trying to decide whether it would be Cannes this summer or not.

I'm pretty sure that was the extent of decision my mother faced during her teenage years. Pretty sure.

She's certainly never known what it is to work.

They relocated to New York in the mid-Eighties, a move that was more escape than escapade; problems went back a long time before we crossed the Atlantic.

I can't really remember because I was young but it seems like I've always known there was an atmosphere, an undercurrent, like the smell of the city on a hot summer's day. There, in the air you breathe. Stinking, with no chance of respite.

No escape, not anywhere, indoors or out.

So I learned to live with it.

When it came to my parents, all New York did was to focus the stench. Until it was too great to ignore.

*   *   *

It started with little things. Like my father staying at the office late. Like having to put myself to bed, the only one in our empty apartment because she was out drinking and he wasn't home from work.

It hadn't always been that way. When we'd first arrived, there'd been a sitter to make sure I didn't get up to any mischief.

That's the way they would have thought of it, too: to stop me getting up to any mischief. Not to make sure I was safe. Not to act as an early warning system.

To keep me out of mischief.

In those early years, my father used to work most weekends.

Then the Eighties really began to happen. And I mean really.

At that time, he was in advertising, ideally placed to feed off the movers and shakers, persuading them to part with money twice – once on pushing products and once again on the products themselves.

Leeches really made the money from those days. Not just the downtown top guns and shoulder-pad girls. In fact, leeches may even have made out better when the collapse came.

By then, though, he'd already made the move to consulting and was telling them how to pick up the pieces and make it big again.

My father and his kind; parasites suckling on the lifeblood of boom and bust.

He had all the status symbols, of course. Porsche. Filofax. Aluminium briefcase. Brick cellphone.

He'd even fly back over to London just to see what the guys in the old hometown were buying. No other reason, I thought, just curiosity.

Didn't occur to me until much later, when I was sleeping in alleyways off Eighth, that there might have been any number of other things he might have been doing on those trips. Women, gambling, a second family, anything.

Aside from Cocaine.

He didn't need to fly to London to do that; never hid it, not around the house.

When I think of my early teenage years, as we settled into the city, I remember him with a white moustache of crystalline white dust.

Photo-flash recollections; memories of wasted time.

*   *   *

Later, when he'd climbed some rungs on the social ladder, we'd weekend on Fire Island, a thin strip of land to the south of Long Island, where it felt like everyone from the city went to relax. Everyone who was anyone, or who wanted to be. By this time, it was more important to be seen there than in the office over the weekend. Almost as if the ultimate status symbol in workaholic times was to be seen not to work.

How many of the summer people lay awake at night, secretly calculating the interest they were paying to lease a pathetic little wooden building on a wannabe island?

The conversations there were scary. People would wax lyrical about the fact that no vehicles were allowed on the island, about how it was *just, like, so natural*; how you could be yourself without any of the pressure of the city.

Well if it was so natural, why did they start eyeing each other up as soon as they walked through the door?

Shoes? Italian. OK.

Wayfarers by Rayban. Cool enough.

If there were no vehicles on the island, why did they start discussing cars the moment they got together?

There were few children on Fire Island, and I had no choice but to observe the adults, listen to their conversations.

To watch what they didn't say.

The way they threw their heads back, laughing at a comment in passing, only to then glare at each others' backs.

And at the centre of the milieu, my parents.

My mother, grinding her teeth whenever he said something. I still don't know if she noticed that he looked at women's breasts when he was talking to them.

So wrapped up in their mutual, cold loathing, the pursuit of material aspiration; I could have drowned on those weekends and they wouldn't have noticed.

And that's not me being dramatic. It's the truth.

It almost happened.

I got flipped by a wave while I was out swimming. They were with all the other sharks, playing on the beach; volleyball or something like that. Likely comparing tans. And me? I was flipping and flopping in the surf. Swallowing water each time I screamed. And I *did* scream. But none of them heard me. Because none of them were watching. No-one was listening.

Except for some guy who ran two hundred yards along the beach before diving into the surf to grab me.

Two hundred yards.

And none of them noticed until he was carrying me out of the water.

Two hundred yards.

I'd forgotten most of this until I was sixteen, until one of my father's colleagues, out of her brain on vodka and cocaine, told me about it.

*   *   *

We're sitting on the bathroom floor, where she's given me a little snort of her coke off the tiles; because I'm cute, she says.

She looks like Linda Kozlowski in Crocodile Dundee *– I'm fighting back a hard-on, thinking of all those movies that had so recently fed my puberty-stricken mind:* Risky Business, Weird Science, The Breakfast Club, Revenge of the Nerds *and any French movie I managed to find on late night TV.*

She keeps giggling and looking at me through her upper eyelashes, bending her head forward and going cross-eyed in the process. Calling me cutie and here's me thinking that all those films – Christ! How could I forget The Graduate? *– are going to come true, that my very own Mrs Robinson is going to set me free right here and now.*

Only she doesn't, she just giggles and says what a bitch my mother is.

And I do a double take.

"A bitch," she says again with spite.

I try to change the subject. "What do you do at Dad's office?"

She bends her head forward, looks up at me again and I'm fighting not to let my eyes drop from hers, knowing that her top is gaping at the neck, that a real, honest-to-God opportunity to see real cleavage is right here in front of me and she's looking me in the eyes.

"You almost drowned," she says, "when we were out on Fire Island."

"Huh?" Now my attention is anywhere but down her top.

"You…" she looks at my face, realises that she's worrying me, "years ago. We were… You… He pulled you out of the sea and you were blue."

She grabs my left hand, the one nearest to her, holds it up as if trying to see the light through it.

"Blue," her voice filled with wonder.

"Really?" I ask and some part of me must remember this because it's not really that great a shock after all. Maybe I just chose not to remember it.

"Yeah," she nods repeatedly, cocaine agreeing with me, "and she didn't even hold you when they brought you up to the house. I thought she's such a bitch because all she said was… All she said when we got back to the house was…"

I nod, trying to get her to spit it out.

"She wanted to know whether the insurance would have covered it."

Doesn't surprise me at all, nothing would when it comes to my mother.

She's still holding my hand in the air.

Her hand is warm.

Her top yawning.

What the hell, I think, I might as well.

I try my best Tom Cruise.

I pout a little, flicker my eyelids like I'm fighting tears, grind my teeth so that the muscle above my jawbone will flex – I'd practised that one for hours in front of the mirror after I'd seen Top Gun.

"What?" she says, suddenly alarmed.

I pout a bit more, shaking a little to add to the effect.

And she puts her arm around me, pulling me close, going shhhhh *over and over again.*

When I reach to touch her tit though, she bursts out laughing.

"You dirty fuck!" she snorts through giggles, "you dirty little fuck!"

I must be blushing red as a stop sign by this point because she just looks at me again and starts laughing even harder.

"You dirty little..."

But she doesn't get anything else out because her nose starts to bleed. The initial drips soon become a constant flow and she looks about herself, all panic and whites of the eyes.

She shoves toilet paper up her left nostril to stem the tide. Blood all down her.

"Fuck! Fuck! Fuck!"

There are red spots all down the front of her top.

Which is probably expensive. Which is probably why she's so angry.

She looks up at me. "Want to grab my fucking tit now, you little bastard?"

I shrug and it just seems to make her even more angry.

I decide to get out of there as quickly as I can.

But she's between me and the door.

"Where do you think you're going?"

"To get some help," I lie.

"Cute," she says, all acid and bile, "very cute."

"Huh?" I'm all innocence.

"Can't wait to get out of here, can you?"

"Huh?"

"To tell them all what happened. Just like your fucking bitch of a mother!" She's spitting the words out, kind of nasal thanks to the toilet paper.

"I should go and get you some help," I say, trying anything I can to get past her and out the door.

By this time, I'm sure people in the apartment must have heard our raised voices.

"No wonder he wants to leave her," she explodes and the paper flies from her nose, dragging a trail of red with it, spatters falling all over the floor and her top and my face.

This seems to take the life out of her.

"Shit," she sighs and crumples to the floor.

"I should go and get you some help," I repeat.

"Yeah, I think you should," she nods, seeming to know the game is up, that there's no way she can avoid the others knowing about this.

"Do you want me to get one of my mother's tops for you?"

The look of gratitude in her eyes is breath-taking. She's probably a power-dressing high priestess during the day and anything that changes that image either in her own or others' eyes is to be avoided at all costs.

"You'd do that?"

For a moment, my mind reels; do I dare, do I really dare?

She's looking at me.

I'm looking at her.

Her nose is dripping blood onto the tiles.

I nod as obviously as possible; staring at blood spreading between the fabric threads covering her chest.

She pulls the roll of toilet paper hard and it spins, a trail of it ruffling up into the air like a streamer. Rips some off and shoves it up her nose for the second time.

We stare at each other.

Blood on the floor has made little spider shapes on impact.

She shrugs.

"OK, but be quick."

She closes her eyes while she lifts one side of her blouse, unhooking her bra to reveal her left breast.

I grab. Feel. Knead. Like it's one of those stress toys my Dad brought home – always lying that it was a present for me as soon as he saw the disappointment in my eyes.

She shudders and I realise with a horrid sense of emptiness that she's not enjoying this at all.

Not like the movies. Not at all. It's just not right.

I let go.

"Something white?" I say.

She opens her eyes, mortified by what she's come to, and nods.

"That'll be fine," and she walks past me without another word. Stands facing the wall, hands active beneath her top, regaining her bra while I leave the bathroom.

I grab one of my mother's tops from their dressing room, hoping – and at the same time knowing – that I won't be spotted, confident that I exist under any radar that might be scanning for me. When I get to the bathroom, I knock on the door. She opens it a crack and I push the top through. She closes the door immediately without a word.

I return to the party.

* * *

Where I was ignored for the rest of the evening. Particularly by my bathroom confidante, who walked straight past me, pecked my father on the cheek and left without another word.

My father didn't seem to notice, too busy discussing interior design and the latest Italian furniture trends or similar with another guy.

My mother was nowhere to be seen.

Nowhere.

So I got drunk on vodka and coke, puked my guts in the bathroom – which had been cleansed of all red spiders – and passed out in my bedroom.

Alone except for memories of the bathroom. None of which got me horny or made me smile.

Chapter 4:
Family Rules – Part I

I was the centre of attention.

Although for the longest time I forgot.

Because I was the centre of attention when I was only a year old.

Everyone loved me. I was the cute kid. The blue eyes, the smirk, the way I lit up anyone's face with the radiance of my own.

The camera loved me.

And everyone who saw me fell a little bit in love.

When I reached out to grasp something, my pudgy little baby hands waving in the air, keen to grasp hold of whatever it was that had caught my attention, it would be in my hands before I even had chance to yell frustration; placed there by some adult whose only purpose was to keep me happy, or so it seemed.

They wanted me.

Look over here.

No, over here.

Coochy-coo.

Do you want your rattle?

This way.

That way.

Smile at me, baby.

Action.

The cameras would roll. The actors would act.

And the child star would do his thing without being able to think about it, without ever *having* to think about it. Smiling, gurgling, winning the audience over with his cobalt blue eyes and huge, gums-only grin.

* * *

Between scenes, they gave me sugar syrup on a spoon.

Kept me happy.

Kept me docile.

I looked forward to the time between scenes more than I did the scenes themselves.

I was one year old.

Chapter 5:
Ivvy

Washington Square was a regular haunt during my lost time.

It was an easy place.

An easy place to score.

An easy place to get lost.

An easy place, despite police who often outnumbered dealers two-to-one, sometimes pretending to be dealers themselves.

Undercover zealots.

There's a thin line between doing the work and becoming just another junkie, though. Even the most fanatical could fall and, when they did, there wasn't even the opportunity to shout for help.

I didn't really see her, not at first. She was just another shadow in a world seeking to avoid the light.

"You look like you've lived," she said.

I wasn't sure whether it was a statement, criticism, question or compliment. People didn't talk to strangers in Washington Square unless they wanted something.

She nodded at me.

"Come on," she urged, "don't give me that strong, silent-type bullshit."

I just stared.

She looked about herself, at the thinning crowds; up at the sky, watching evening draw in.

Sighed.

About thirty, although in the evening's fading light I might have been wrong.

"You live here?" she asked.

I shook my head, tired of trying to catch her eye just so I could stare her out.

"Tourist?"

I shook my head, scanned the square.

She was looking at me now, her head cocked a little in the late evening shadows; sun falling behind tenements and sky-scrapers, bringing dusk to the park early.

"You don't live here but you're not visiting?" She sounded cynical. And tired.

I was beginning to enjoy this game.

Beginning to enjoy myself.

In the city, *'here'* is always New York, and someone was either from *'here'* or not.

Which, given my background, was why I could answer either way.

"Yup," I said with a slight smile.

She watched shadows chase up the red-brick of the university.

Shivered.

Summer and she was shivering despite the humidity. I knew that feeling.

"So which is it?"

"Both," I said, a faux enigma, as mysterious as a twelve year old goth explaining how The Cure are, like, you know, *rilly* deep.

She burst out laughing.

I had to laugh a little myself.

Smiling, I turned to face her; she mirrored me.

Reached out her hand.

"Ivvy," she said.

I thought I'd misheard her. My father said *iffy* all the time.

"Huh?"

"Ivvy," she said, again proffering her hand, and I realised it must be her name.

So I held out my hand, went to shake hers.

Like a cobra, she had me, pulling my arm towards her, twisting my wrist to reveal my inner arm.

She smiled at the small scattering of track-marks.

"Told you," she said, vindicated.

"Huh?"

"That you've lived," she continued, smiling her victory, "I knew it! Now what's your name?"

"Reggie," I said, regaining my hand, standing to leave.

"Reggie?" she repeated as if she'd never heard the name before.

"Reggie," I was back to staring her out.

After close-calls with make-believe dealers, searching for their commendation and medal, I'd decided that every week would see a different me visit the Square. Reggie was the name I was using that week.

There had been something about the way she had grabbed my arm.

"What precinct are you with?" I smiled like a threatened cross-breed.

She spread her hands, palms up.

"That obvious?"

"That obvious."

She looked about herself; left, right, near, far.

But we were alone among seven million people.

And she slid up her sleeve.

Bruises.

Small and large all the way up her forearm; calligraphy of addiction.

"Amazing what they can do with make-up isn't it?" My distrust knew no bounds.

It was impossible to read any emotion in her face. I could see only the cold calculation of how she was going to corner me, get me to confess, to incriminate myself and others.

Taxis and buses taunted each other in the distance, all blaring horns and revving engines. Subway trains sent seismic shimmers through the concrete.

And before I knew it, she was opening a wrap, dipping her finger in and rubbing it on her teeth. Like the oldest cliché in the book.

"Want some?" she asked.

It was my turn to scan the park to see if we were being watched.

Left, right, near, far, up, down, doorways, windows, fire escapes.

"Well?" She pushed me.

"Put it away will you?"

"You don't want some?"

"I don't do…"

"Yeah, like fuck you don't!" She spluttered laughter and I decided it best to be elsewhere, turning and walking; downtown, towards Soho.

Through the monolithic NYU campus.

Stepping over street-sleepers already crashed out in the gutter.

Which brought back memories of a dead body; the night B.B. King sang the park to sleep.

Walking. Not looking back.

Not turning to check whether I was being followed.

Until I crossed Houston, turning west. I sensed her right behind me; realized I'd had that feeling since I'd left the Square.

It was only when I was walking down the steps into Spring Street subway that she spoke to me, such a surprise that I almost stopped breathing.

"You're not worth it, buddy boy," she said, voice suddenly hard as granite, "unless you can help me score. It's not that easy for me, catch my drift?"

I didn't say a word. This was serious. She was far, far off orders.

She grabbed my arm, spinning me to face her.

"I said *do you catch my drift?*"

I tried to tell her that I did, I really did.

Only I was spinning on the step and losing my balance and tumbling backwards. Walls became ceiling, steps became walls, all of it blurring as I fell down Spring Street stairs. Bumping, bruising; what felt like broken bones on each jarring impact.

"Fuck!" I heard her yell over the sounds of my own grunts and moans.

I was gone for a moment. In the comfort of the black.

Next thing I knew, the world had settled back to normality. I could taste blood. The ceiling was back where it should be.

She was leaning over me, checking me out.

Someone kicked my ribs as they tried to step over me. I gave a little yelp because I hadn't breath enough to scream.

"Watch out, you fucker!" she shouted at my temporary assailant, then to me, "Jesus! D'ya get these people?"

"I..."

Before I could say another word, my need to breathe and her adrenalin got the better of me.

"Nothing's broken," she said, voice quick, a machine gun stutter of words, "you seemed to bounce pretty well and it really wasn't that far anyway... Jeez, I'm sorry that I... Are you breathing okay, that's the only thing I can't check... If you've broken a rib... Damn! If you've punctured your lung then, you've gotta tell me..."

"I'm fine," I gasped. While it hurt to do so, I could at least breathe. I tasted blood where I had bitten my tongue.

"Help me up," I ordered.

"Sure?"

"Sure."

She hooked her hands under my armpits.

"On three," she said, "One... Two... Three."

And together we lifted my aching bones to their feet.

This time I did scream.

"Shhhhh..." her calming voice.

She circled me, looking me up and down, making sure that I wasn't about to collapse in a heap on the ground.

I wasn't.

We stared at each other.

Not knowing whether to smile, laugh, cry, shout or scream.

Finally, she reached out both hands and planted them on my shoulders. Gently.

"Junkies of the world unite, eh?" she smiled.

"Guess you could say that," I replied, smiling myself.

"You wanna celebrate?" She patted her pocket.

I nodded.

"Come on then," she said and dropped her hands from my shoulders to hook one arm through mine.

She turned us around and led back up the stairs, each step a cacophony of aches and grimaces. We emerged into the full dark.

"Just one thing," I said, "your name's Ivvy, right?"

"Yup," she replied.

"What the fuck is that all about, then?"

* * *

We trawled the Village, Chelsea and Soho, doing anything we could to avoid the storm cloud brooding low on a horizon. Beyond it only the fix awaited.

"It's short," she said, "short for..."

And left me hanging like the junkie I was.

"Well?" I coerced.

"Ivana," she said, smiling.

"Ivana?"

"Ivana."

I looked her in the eyes, assessing whether she was being serious.

"No, really," I challenged, "Ivana? Really?"

She smiled. Nodded.

"Like Trump? Like that Ivana?"

She touched my forearm and shook her head.

"In name only," she said, "name only."

"What is it, Russian?" I asked.

"Romanian, third generation."

"Oh."

"Ivana," I laughed, smiling to myself, "Ivana…"

*   *   *

Back at her apartment, we smoked weed and did some lines.

I wished that it was smack, even though I was nearing the end of my relationship with that particular mistress.

The street was dry, she said, had been for weeks.

She showed me her badge.

She showed me her uniform.

Ivvy: a naughty teenager, caught outside the school gates. Playing away. Flouting the rules. Running the risk. Understanding too well the laws of demand and supply.

Her straw hair had been blonde once upon a time, she could well have been someone's homecoming queen.

Once upon a time.

Once upon a times.

Aren't we all living off them?

Aren't we all full of shit?

Chapter 6: Believer

There was a time when I believed.

I believed love was love.

I believed that when someone told me I was fantastic, they meant it. That when the photographer told me the camera loved me, then he was besotted by association; audience twice as much again.

I believed that, because I had been on television week-in, week-out for the first five years of my life, people would remember me; still caring for Walter, the cute kid from *Family Rules!*

Like crap they would.

I appeared on talk shows! On my own. At four years of age. Smiling and being cute. Chatting with the host like an old friend.

Two years' later, I was no-one.

And my parents, those so-called elders and betters, couldn't handle it.

So they moved away from the UK.

Moved to the USA.

Moved me to the USA.

They've never told me whether it was an honest attempt to start again; for my sake, their sakes or a little bit of both. To do so would have involved talking with me, having an honest-to-God, down-to-earth conversation; more than just a nod in passing.

My parents don't do conversation.

Not with me.

Once I came off *Family Rules!* they moved our little, broken, three piece suite of a family to America, leaving my manager and agent wondering where it had all gone wrong, where they'd missed a chance, where they might have cut some different deal, where their next meal was coming from.

My parents. Didn't care about me when I was making money, even less when I wasn't. They weren't pushy, stage-parents. If anything, the complete opposite.

Here they were, living the eighties to the hilt, spending her money while he cut his teeth in the advertising business. He scaled the cliff from creative floor to project management to key account executive to Managing Director while his one and only son lived the first five years of his life on television.

Both of us growing up in public.

Bastard.

I'm pretty sure that the move to the States was triggered purely by the potential for embarrassment that I represented once my star had faded.

Too many dinner parties where they could suddenly be asked: *Aren't you little Walter's parents? Whatever happened to him?*

Like I was an object they had misplaced when they were kids.

Like they would even know what my character's name was.

I think they got tired of shrugging their shoulders and reciting well rehearsed lines.

He's a delicate soul... Suffering from the schedule, you know... We really want him to have a normal upbringing...

Yeah, right.

For that, read:

Ken's tantrums are getting out of hand, he cut himself with a knife last week when we told him 'no'... Ken's exhibiting signs of depression... He's only five, but his therapist is suggesting we might want to get him checked out for schizophrenia, which could explain the mood swings... We don't like the fact that you're asking these questions, so we're going to avoid them by moving to America... No-one knows Ken there... At least there we won't be so distracted by him...

My parents; a model of caring and nurture. For themselves.

They ripped apart my belief system for the sake of their social circles.

I was loved.

I believed I was loved.

The love dwindled.

I thought it was me. My fault.

They thought it was me. My fault.

No-one told me otherwise.

They just moved me to America.

As punishment for letting love die.

For losing my belief.

My parents.

Chapter 7:
The Thrill is Gone

I lay on a bench in Washington Square one night, wrapped in desolation.

A wino was crashed out two or three benches along. There had been a minor scuffle earlier, when another guy tried to take his pitch. Little more than hair pulling, slapping and drunken, missed punches, but more than enough to bring my situation home to me.

I was tired, hadn't eaten for a couple of days and didn't know what I was going to do about the mess I was in.

I was scared.

It had been two weeks since I'd walked out of my parents' apartment.

Two weeks. A pitifully short time to grow so despondent. I felt like I'd been alone for a lifetime.

Which, given my parents, was closer to the truth than I cared to admit.

Across the square, a drug deal was going down and I was sure it must have been a set-up, it was so blatant. But there were no flashing lights, no blaring sirens, no S.W.A.T. team dashing from shadows to take them out.

They faded away into the night, rejoining the gloom.

My misery deepened as I lay on the bench.

It was Spring, warm enough to stay out most nights; not like Winter, when my breath felt like it might freeze in my throat. Despite the evening's warmth, though, it might as well have been ice, desperation and hypothermia, I felt so wretched.

Lying in the darkness, the wino snoring, dealers coasting, awaiting their next buyer, I was so close to tears it made me shudder.

Then it came from a stereo in an upstairs apartment, a minor chord drifting across the square like a whisper.

A guitar, electric.

B. B. King.

Unmistakable.

Soft horns in the background; Lucille lifting the darkness for a moment.

'The Thrill is Gone' filled Washington Square.

Everyone was still.

Shadows within shadows grew apparent, people I hadn't even known were there, some of them sniffing back tears, some just humming along.

The guy three benches along woke up and railed at the apartment window: *"Shut the fuck up, we're trying to sleep down here!"*

A rock came out of the darkness and hit his shoulder.

B. B. played on regardless.

By the end of the first chorus, some of the shadows were singing.

Me, I turned over and let the music soothe me to sleep.

B.B. King's guitar melted the night into ice cream and shadows.

I dreamt of twirling carousels and red fairy lights, screaming wheels and ozone bitterness, of the yelps and screams of teenage girls; rough answers from over-protective boyfriends, all bravado and testosterone. My dreams left me spinning, dizzy with vertigo and confusion.

When I woke, in the early hours of dawn, the guy two or three benches along had been knifed and I was the only person within twenty yards of him.

*   *   *

I couldn't move.

I stared at him.

Blood pooled under the bench hadn't had chance to dry as yet; glistening as it congealed in the early daylight.

I looked about myself quickly but there was no-one near me, no-one to offer a hand or respond to a call for help. I could have been the only man in New York City.

I felt like crying, like shouting, like screaming at the top of my lungs.

I DO NOT WANT TO SEE THIS!

I craved silence. Cars revving, buses roaring down Sixth, the bitching of some woman shrieking razor blades through my ear drums, all of it battered me senseless. I couldn't help but stare at this guy, his tongue poking out of a distorted grin, slaver down his chin. Tinged red.

There was no sign of a knife.

Like most winos in the city, he'd been wearing layers, even during this warm period. The bench was surrounded by his plastic bags, shopping cart a few feet away, turned over on one side. All manner of junk had scattered across the pavement.

His collected crap, his life's work, his life's worth spilled on the concrete.

Like his blood.

I coughed a little, tasting bile in my throat.

What should I do now?

I looked about myself again, hoping a cop would be walking by, that I could get rid of this responsibility, this duty, this...

I only woke up next to the guy!

Panic made my breath short and I caught the smell of him over the undercurrent stench of the city. How I wished that backdrop were now like it was in July or August, almost solid in the back of my throat. If it had been, I would have been less able to smell the old wine, sweat, fumes and gasoline trapped in his unwashed hair; grime embedded in his face, his dirty hands, grit under his fingernails. I sniffed hard, testing whether it was my imagination or whether I could actually smell his congealing blood.

It wasn't make-believe.

I was not imagining it.

I could smell his blood.

Because it was on me. Somehow it was on me.

I looked down and my jeans were covered. It had splashed up from where my shoes had stepped in it. Spattered all down the front of my shirt in spots and streaks, some tiny, little more than pin-pricks, some larger; dimes, nickels and quarters in polka-dots across my waist and thighs.

For a moment, I wondered whether I had done this to him.

I couldn't have.

I was sober. I was clean. I would have remembered. Wouldn't I?

I'd have remembered.

Surely?

On the pavement, footsteps from his bench to mine.

They stopped at the point where I'd put my feet up on the bench.

My hands were sticky. I looked at them.

Looked long and hard.

My eyes swam. Bile surged. I doubled over and what little food was left in my stomach came burning up my throat. I retched and retched until I was heaving dryness; catching a quick glimpse of him, his staring, dry eyes, the flies lighting on his neck where... I puked again, even though there was nothing left to come up.

His throat had been cut.

I couldn't have. I couldn't.

I would have remembered. Surely, I'd have remembered.

I looked around myself, now desperate that no-one was there to see this, that the nearest human being be anywhere but in the city, anywhere but running towards Washington Square right that minute.

And that was when I saw it.

It took me a couple of seconds to make sure I wasn't imagining it. Could have been the morning light. Could have been that my eyes were still hazy from sleep. Could have been the tears that had sprung unexpected at the sight of his gaping throat; bloody red smile and staring eyes. It could have been all of these things. Or it could have been what it was, an inverted shadow on my bench, the shape of me asleep on the wood, outlined by blood spatters.

My dream came crashing back to me. The carousel, draped in red light, illuminations flickering. His body reeling while they pushed him between themselves. Of girls screaming and twirling as metal ground against metal; his shrieking fear at the sight of the knife. The rough shouts of the boyfriends, his attackers. The panic; manic chaos, spattering the night with red light and insult.

And all the time, I'd been laying there like the world's biggest piece of toothbrush art, like some toddler was having the greatest laugh of its life, spattering me with red paint, outlining me against the green and grey wood of the bench.

Now I was able to breathe, I could see that the footprints leading to my bench had been left by boots. I was wearing sneakers.

One of them had walked over to check I was crashed out.

I was suddenly flooded with relief. I had not killed the guy.

I hadn't killed him.

I had just watched while they did; possibly a greater evil.

Before I knew it, I was running.

I almost tore my shirt off as I went. But then I remembered what forensics could do. I turned it inside out, resolving to burn it later.

That done, I ran. And ran.

And ran.

*   *   *

Blissful ignorance, regular Joes and Josephines, heading out for their first coffee of the morning; voluntary blindness for just another wino, running down the road and cursing under his breath.

I ran.

Until I was in the middle of nowhere. Or what passed for it in New York: Central Park. Over the bridge that spanned the boating lake, into the wilderness of the rambles. Under some trees, I grabbed a bag of clothes from another rough-sleeper, crashed out on a bench.

A few minutes further away, I took stock of the clothes. There was a jacket in the bag that didn't look too bad. Some trousers too but I stopped short of putting them on. The jacket would be enough.

I headed north, more than aware that that the park wasn't safe but keen to avoid the streets. Police preferred asphalt to undergrowth at that time of morning.

I needed to burn my clothes but had no idea where I could do that. Unless...

A million clichéd movie scenes flooded my mind.

I knew where to go.

*   *   *

I stood at the east river, longing for stereotypical movie sets, for a winter's night and a trashcan filled with glowing coals and flame;

in the middle of May, I had as much chance of that happening as my mother caring enough to kiss things better. With no hope of burning my clothes, I decided to put time between myself and the murder. I sat in an alleyway, disguised by trash, and waited for dark.

Despite it all, my vigil was tinged with a growing sense of excitement.

His body would have been discovered early that morning. There was no way it would have gone unnoticed. A dead body was a dead body, bad for business no matter what the business may have been. Whether it was police or junkie who found him, it would have been called in almost immediately. Which means they'd have completely searched the area. Which means they'd have worked out that there was someone sleeping on the third bench along who must have been covered in blood and probably knew a good deal about what had happened, who might even have had a hand in it.

I had hours to run the scenes and script through my imagination.

With each hour that passed, I grew more and more convinced that I was in the clear.

Sure, in my panic I had walked much of Manhattan that morning, variously visible in blood stained trousers and shirt, or liberated jacket. Were they to have put out a dragnet, released photo-montage images of my possible face, or gone door-to-door across the whole island, they might just have been able to trace my journey.

But they wouldn't have. Because he was only another bum, crashed out in the village. The city tolerated its victims provided they remained below radar, offering unseen hand-outs and soup kitchens; acts of denial for the collective guilty conscience. Just another bum.

The screenplay started over again; the movie gaining depth with each virtual performance.

I continued to grow excited as I huddled amongst newspaper sheets soaked in pig-blood; meat district packing.

If they were looking for me, they hadn't found me yet and wouldn't if I stayed right there. The more time passed, the better the chance I had.

They would be looking for me in the village.

I was nowhere near.

By evening, I was locked in the rapture of an escaped convict. Since waking to find a dead body not fifteen feet from where I'd slept, I had suspected myself of murder, stolen from people who had nothing and sequestered myself beneath obnoxious garbage. I felt good. Excited. Elated.

Like shouting: *Nyah-nyah, you can't catch me!*

I couldn't contain my energy – it was time to move.

I ripped my blood-stained shirt into strips and distributed them across alleyways before scattering the remainder into the East River. After that, wearing my lice-ridden, knock-off finery, I walked back towards the Square.

I wanted to see what had happened.

And the thought of being back there gave me a pure adrenalin rush; my own return to the lion's den.

*   *   *

For the first time in a long time, I felt a high without having to inject or ingest a single chemical. And, though I didn't know it at the time, it was the birth of a new addiction for me.

Flirting with the law, playing cat and mouse with the NYPD.

I walked into Washington Square feeling the rush of a very new thrill.

My new fix.

Chapter 8:
Family Rules – Part II

Martin Sanderson was fifty-two years old when they pitched him the pilot of *Family Rules!*

For about ten years, he'd been living at the bottom of a bottle of scotch, drinking desperately in the hope of rescuing the drowning remnants of his career; if he could just get them above the surface, he might be able to resuscitate them, pull them together, make them mean more together than they had as tatters for the last decade. If only he could get his act together.

If only.

If only.

And then the script had arrived.

The motorbike messenger handed him the clipboard. "Sign there."

As normal, Sanderson watched for any sign of recognition. Nothing. Not even a glimmer.

Probably too young to remember *Charge Squad*, the police drama series that had made him a star a decade earlier. Did memories really fade as quickly as that?

He closed the door on the messenger and looked at the package. A script, without doubt.

The postmark was enough to tell him that it wasn't even from his agent, who had long since relegated him to the *used-to-be-but-aren't-now* pile. Sanderson's denial had been so blind drunk that he'd only realised this after several years without a phone call or a letter.

The envelope was ripped open before he'd even got into his living room.

He settled in to read.

*   *   *

If only Sanderson had known that it was all a vehicle for Jamie Master's first foray into television, he might have thought differently. But they didn't sell it like that. Too sharp to fall into the honesty trap. Too sharp by half.

"Hello, is that Rodney? Er... Mr Blythe?"

"No, this is his office."

His office, he thought, *she actually said his office.*

Stifling a cynical laugh at the image of a speaking building, he continued on.

"Is Mr Blythe in the office?"

"Hold on," she said, voice fading away from the other end of the phone and then suddenly back, loud in his ear. "Who's speaking please?"

"It's Martin Sanderson," he replied, "Mr Blythe sent me a copy of *Family Rules!* to consider and I'm just following up. Can you tell me if..."

"Martin Sanderson?"

He smiled. She'd recognised his name. It still thrilled him, never tiring of the adoration.

"Yes," he said, smiling warmth down the wire, balancing between patronising her and letting her bask in his sunlight, "that's right."

"Good. He's been waiting for you to call."

Waiting for me to call. Waiting... For... Me... To... Call...

"Really?"

"Yup. He's been speaking to Chris Owen in the meantime. Calling you all manner of... What? Hang on a sec."

She muffled the phone with one hand to speak with someone at the far end. Finally she came back.

"My mum's going to be so pleased I talked to you," she said, "she used to watch you when I was growing up... OK, OK, OK... Jesus, he's such a slave-driver!"

And then she reverted to the chirpy receptionist she was paid to be.

"Just putting you through," she said, voice brimming with autonomic affectation, devoid of personality.

The line buzzed and clicked as she patched the call.

"Hello," a gruff voice, impatient, intolerant of delay, "Rodney Blythe."

"Ah yes, Mr Blythe it's Mar..."

"Call me Rodney, I ain't got time for anything else."

"Right... Rodney. Rodney. Rodney..."

"Like the sound of that? Or have you got something you actually want to talk about?"

Snapping back to reality.

"It's Martin Sanderson here," he said, "you sent me..."

"I know what I sent you, what do you think?"

"Huh?"

"Well it's not as if you've had an agent check it out first, is it?"

"Huh?"

"Look Martin, the world, his wife and several mistresses on separate continents know that your career's gone so far south it's fucking penguins, so let's just drop the pretence, OK? I sent you the script because no agent was willing to act as a go between. Dealing with the talent. I hate it. Literally hate it. Talent. Fuck!"

Sanderson didn't know what to say. If he'd been able to draw breath, he might have spluttered, but he couldn't even do that.

"So, as I say, let's not play games with each other, eh?" Blythe continued. "What I'm offering you is a chance to get back on prime-time again. You remember prime-time, don't you?"

"Yes," he answered involuntarily.

"Good. So what do you think?"

"What?"

"Like I say, no time for pissing around. Are you in or not?"

"Or you'll go for Chris Owen, right?" under his breath, hoping he wouldn't be heard.

"He's already signed on," Blythe was smiling at the other end of the phone, you could hear it in his voice.

"What do you mean? I thought we were up for the same part?"

"You what?"

"Chris and I... We're up for Michael, aren't we?"

A loud guffaw buzzing through the wires.

"Michael? *Michael?* Do you really think you're being considered for a thirty-five year old father? For fuck's sake, you're fifty seven if you're a day, how the fuck did you think... You're down for Michael's father. His father."

His father.

An infirm old man forced to live his life with his son and young family.

Sanderson grimaced at the handset, his face white.

"All right," he said quietly, knowing when he was beaten.

"All right, we'll talk about rates tomorrow. I need to speak to Jamie first to make sure she's okay with this."

"Jamie?"

"Masters."

The topless model from *The Sun*?

"Jamie Masters?"

"Quick on the uptake, ain't ya speedy?"

"Jamie Masters, the page-three girl? *That* Jamie Masters?"

"Yup, *that* Jamie Masters. She's our long-suffering heroine."

Sanderson's eyes rolled up in his sockets, eyelids fluttering down for a moment as he contemplated this latest left-turn.

He swallowed the lump in his throat.

"Good," he said, eyes still closed, "speak to you tomorrow."

And hung up the phone.

A topless tart and the latest hunk of beefcake taking top billing and leaving him, Martin Sanderson, a trained Shakespearian actor, relegated to playing a sick old man forced to rely on his family for food and water.

How far things had come since *Charge Squad*; how deep the trench into which he had sunk.

He lifted the glass of Bells scotch that had been by his side throughout the phone call and held it aloft.

"Here's to you Jamie," he said by way of a toast and then added, with a sigh, "and here's to a great set of tits on-set."

Chapter 9:
De Nada

My parents and I didn't talk that much. We were ships that didn't even sail the same sea; they left port in the morning, me in the twilight hours.

In my teenage years, I had more conversation with Oliveria, the cleaner, than with my mother or father.

When I turned nineteen, she gave me a little bracelet with my name inscribed: *Ken*. Not Kenneth, not Kenny, not Walter. Ken. It was wrapped in colourful wrapping paper, a flower-and-leaf print that reminded me of old people; the light blue box within was unmistakable, though. Tiffany's.

She didn't have to buy me anything.

But she had.

A tear began to swell in my eye. The last time I'd got a real birthday present from my mother or father, when they'd actually gone out and spent time browsing the shops, trying to work out just what would make me happy, had been when we were still in the UK. Even then, I'd have been surrounded by my entourage – the Manager, the Agent, the Producer, the Director and all the other hangers on – so my memories could well be lies. Almost definitely, I would guess.

Any affection they have ever shown has been dictated by my therapists.

Oliveria had taken the time though.

It wasn't as if Oliveria could claim to have become a virtual member of the family. My parents rarely spent time speaking with her, let alone getting to know her. That would take more than a moment of not being selfish; impossible for them, simply impossible.

"For me?" I asked and realised immediately that it was the most corny thing I could have said, patronising her despite her honest gesture.

She simply nodded her head at the Tiffany box, ordering me to open it.

The bracelet lay on a foam pad, nameplate upwards.

Ken.

My heart choked my throat; tears coming now, unstoppable.

"Ken," she said, nodding, "it is your name. *Su nombre.*"

"I don't understand," I said. "Why?"

"Why what?" She shrugged.

But I couldn't get a word out, my throat constricted, dry, making it impossible to swallow.

"Shhh..." she said, guiding my hand to the bracelet, "put it on."

Where she led, I followed and the gift was soon on my wrist. She looked at it for a long while. Eventually, she nodded for a final time and fixed my eyes with a stare, her dark eyes suddenly voluminous.

"*Su nombre,*" she said, voice quiet, "*no lo olvide.*"

And she was turning around and walking away and I was left in the kitchen, wondering how she could have afforded this, why she had been willing to afford it, why the present, why the message, why she...

"Oliveria!" I shouted and was on my feet before I could think about it.

She turned and I was on her in an instant, hugging her tight and sobbing into her shoulder.

She didn't say anything for a long time. Not until the sobs had dwindled, not until her shoulder was soaked with my tears.

"Why?" I asked, voice muffled in the material of her housecoat.

She didn't reply.

"Why?" Again, more insistent.

She pulled back and looked me in the eyes again, shaking her head slightly.

"*De nada,*" she said, "*nada.*"

And this time she did leave, regaining her coat and bag on the way up the hall, closing the door without looking back to see whether I was watching, following or collapsing in a heap on the ground.

That's how I remember my nineteenth birthday.

What a way to recall it; tears and mystery, jewellery and a moment's solace.

*   *   *

About two weeks before Bella, I came home to find my parents sharing the dining table, sharing a meal. Even sharing a conversation; unusual enough to make the memory very clear.

He was at the head of the table, her a couple of seats down one side.

A Matisse hung over the fireplace, some obscure piece likely to be desired by every museum and gallery in the world. They had bought it on a whim in Paris about ten years previously. She'd liked the colours. That's what she'd said, *I like the colours*, and it had been bought within the hour. They might as well have bought an empty frame and hung it there for how much they looked at the Matisse once it was hung in the apartment. They rarely sat to eat in this room.

Even though their meal was unusual, I wasn't really interested enough to listen to their discussion. I was passing towards the kitchen to find something to gnaw on when he called out to me.

"Ken," he said and then paused, waiting until I turned around.

I wondered whether I should give him the satisfaction.

"Ken," he said again, by way of confirmation that there was no choice.

So, I turned to look at him. Despite the imperative, he wouldn't meet my gaze, turning instead to look at my mother who, in turn, scrutinized her half empty plate like it was a photograph developing in a darkroom.

This wasn't their normal abnormality. Something was up.

He coughed, quietly but enough to make his point.

"Your…" she started to speak, unsure of how to move forward, "your… Grandfather has… He died, Kenneth. Your Grandfather is dead."

My father chased a potato around his plate.

"Really?" I asked, trying to put some emotion in my voice, trying to recall the few acting lessons I'd had towards the end of *Family Rules!* when they'd finally realised that I was speaking more than Chris or Martin, that I was becoming pivotal to the comedy on-screen and the drama off.

Now she looked at me; her stare could freeze mercury in an instant.

"Don't give me that," she said, hissing, "don't you dare act like… Like…"

"I…"

"You have never met him," she said, speaking the truth we all knew too well.

Not as if it was my fault that her family didn't meet but once a year, when they held their family summit at a lakeside chateau near Lausanne. To which the kids, cousins I hadn't met, weren't invited unless they were investment bankers doing something productive to further the family fortune, not denude it like me.

I'd never been to Switzerland.

Never been to the family summit.

Never met my Grandfather.

Why should I care? I thought.

The silence in the room was so dense that I began to wonder if I'd said it out loud. They both watched space rather than me, rather than each other.

I was still hungry.

"So?" I asked, more to break the stalemate than wanting to know why they felt it necessary to tell me.

My father was the one to answer the question, my mother seeming to realise she'd been further outside her shell in the previous few minutes than in many years; frosty exterior breached, even if only for the shortest moment.

"We have to go to the funeral," he answered.

"Well, duh..." I couldn't help myself. Neither of them even rose to the bait.

"We *have* to go to the funeral," he repeated and I suddenly realised that he wasn't actually talking to me but to her instead. And that one sentence, the emphasis, the imperative... She didn't want to go. She didn't want to have to go.

Funerals engendered emotion, and she didn't do emotion, not at all. It was so straightforward. So simple.

So typical.

That was why they'd been sitting there, having dinner when most nights he was out drinking while she was out comparing fashion notes with the Upper East crones. He would have suggested they talk it through because somewhere in one of his management consulting books, in some easily forgotten paragraph in some hotel room somewhere, he'd read that it was important to talk through issues.

Totally ignoring that his whole marriage had been based upon avoiding that sort of sound advice.

That night, she'd have been fighting him tooth and nail that they weren't going and he'd have been pushing back. Which made me wonder why he was suddenly so concerned that they do the right thing about a member of either of their families.

Probably worried that she'd be cut out of the estate.

Probably.

I decided to twist the knife, bloody from where they'd been stabbing each other all evening.

"Do you want me to come?" I asked.

They both turned and looked at me, speaking in unison, voices flat, hard, not a single emotion for me to grab hold of.

"No."

I looked at them, they looked at avoidance. And the conversation was over.

I went to get some food.

*   *   *

The next day, I tumbled out of bed a little before noon to find a note on the kitchen counter, written in his hand.

> *Further to our discussion, we've gone to your Grandfather's funeral. We'll be gone for a month or so.*

And that was it. No signature. No *'look after yourself'*. No *'see you later'*. No *'we'll call when we arrive'* Nothing.

I went back to bed.

*   *   *

If you ask me whether the lack of real affection in my family had anything to do with Bella, with what happened, I'd have to tell you that I don't know. On the surface, maybe.

Maybe.

One thing I know for certain, though. Below that surface, the water is deep.

Chapter 10:
Trade

Ivvy and I wandered through Soho, one of our many days spent browsing shops in which we never intended to spend a dime. Wondering what people saw in all these belongings, what my parents saw in them.

Ivvy; her blonde, ratty hair, cropped to the nape of her neck. Every so often, choreographed for some imagined movie scene, all subtle lighting and angles, she tossed her head, flipping her hair from left to right or vice versa. On virtual celluloid, the sun filtered through her hair, glowing through strands, adding a halo as she flicked her fringe. Reality told a different story; straw on her head frizzing a little as static, humidity and city grime conspired to add weight where it was unwanted.

"What is it you do exactly?" I asked her, looking in the Prada shop and wondering whether it was even worth entering; we'd been thrown out within four minutes the last time we'd stepped in, politely followed by some male model between engagements but a good enough coat hanger on which to drape the product.

"You know," she chided, not slowing a jot.

"No," I replied truly ignorant, "I mean, I know you're something in the good old NYPD blue, but you've never told me what."

"I haven't?" Now she knew she was stringing me along, the note of her voice changing as she began to play with me.

"No, you haven't."

She didn't say anything for a few minutes and I wondered whether the conversation was closed.

"You're not gonna freak out, right?" she said eventually.

"Right."

She stopped, turned to face me.

"You mean it, right?"

"Yeah. Said so, didn't I?"

Ivvy nodded, looked up and down the street, checked no-one was in listening distance; even looked above us, checking the fire escapes, windows and roof gardens.

Like the first time we'd met, in Washington Square.

"I'm a hooker," she said.

It stopped me dead.

"You're what?"

"A hooker."

"But... But you... I thought you were with the pol..."

"I am."

I did a double take and it was clear she understood my confusion; playing with me still.

"Undercover," she said quietly, again checking up and down the street.

"Really?" I was impressed; this was unexpected to say the least.

She nodded.

"But I..."

This time she laughed. "Jesus Christ, Ken! It's not as if I just told you I'm a pro for real!"

"It's not that," I fired back, "it's just… How do they let you get away w…"

"When I'm on the street, I'm watching, making notes, sometimes wear a wire."

"Who are you after, the pros or the punters?"

"Punters?"

"The guys… Look, it's something my father says, all right!"

"Take it easy, man! Easy. I just hadn't heard it before, that's all. Jeez! Usually it's the guys who cruise the girls we're after, the… punters. The pimps if we can get them."

"My respect knows no bounds," I said, still smarting from her reaction Although I wanted my voice to drip sarcasm, it actually came out sounding pretty much like a compliment.

She laughed at me again.

"It's not that amazing," she said, "it's just what I do. Most of the time I'm just freezing my ass off in the snow or sweating in the heat."

"I was being sarcastic," I said, choosing transparency's best tactic.

"I know," she smiled, punching my arm.

"Show me how you do it?" I asked.

"What?"

"How you do it," I repeated, "I want to see."

"Do what?"

"Act like a hooker… I want to see it."

She looked around herself, at the streets of Soho, busy as usual on this Spring day.

"Here?" Her voice was filled with disbelief and ridicule.

"It's a street isn't it?"

I walked over to a low window ledge; sat down, leaning forward, arms on knees.

Expectant.

"Go on."

"No."

"Go on."

"You're kidding, right?"

I shook my head. Ivvy looked up and down the street, at the faces of people passing by, bumping her shoulder as they passed, banging her shins with shopping bags, briefcases and folded coats.

Her eyes contained something like panic.

"Not exactly the right neighbourhood," she said, nodding at the seething street.

Music erupted from a shop up the road as someone pushed the door open; reggae, pulsing sub-bass and stabbing horns. Sex on vinyl.

"They're playing your song," I said and smiled at her.

"You really want me to?" Her voice was full of disappointment.

I just smiled.

Without another word, Ivvy walked off up the street.

"Ivvy!" I shouted after her.

She just raised the back of her right hand above her shoulder, dismissing me with a single gesture. A single finger.

Once again, I was alone in the foaming sea of the city. Suddenly all those briefcase boys and Chanel girls were too close to me, not just passing by on the street. Aftershave and perfume cut the stench of the city; acid-washed and scrubbed, these exfoliated, effervescent, excessive urban executives. Their path peppered by the underclass; raggedy pants and t-shirts, sweat and cheap wine halitosis.

All of them. Too close to me.

I would have held my breath if I thought it would stop the oppressive weight of the city. But it wasn't just a smell thing; New York assailed all senses in every way imaginable twenty-four-seven.

I had only been joking.

Surely she'd known that?

I was joking!

She'd done this sort of thing before; queen of the unpredictable mood swing. It was the come-down, or her period, or some medical condition I could have learnt about if I'd been bothered. The previous week, it had been storming out of Macy's because I hadn't said she looked good in a little red skirt she'd been trying on. The week before that, when she hadn't wanted to eat at Burger King. Just like now, she hadn't said a word, she'd just walked. It was something of a normal occurrence when I spent time with Ivvy.

I decided to watch the crowd instead, the river of blood, bone and breath flowing before my eyes.

Hot women, square-jawed management wannabes, fatties pulling hard on *Big Gulps*, chomping down on burgers, chins drizzled with grease, execs stepping sideways to avoid black guys, confirming every stereotype in a single movement.

I only became aware of the change over the course of five minutes.

There was nothing spectacular, nothing different, no sound or signal but I sensed the shift in the focus of the street as soon as it moved. It was in the way they paused a little as they walked in front of me, slowing their pace; a few more collisions, heavier breathing. When I looked up, more of them were looking away from where I sat. They were looking...

Across the street.

She was on the corner, bag dangling from her left forearm, hips kicked out to the right, hand planted securely there. The top she'd been wearing a few minutes earlier was now ripped.

Ivvy: every inch a caricature.

A group of young guys out for lunch came between me and the corner where she was standing as clear as a billboard.

I leant to my right to try and see around them. But they were too dense, too many, and I lost her. They joked with each other, a couple of them pointing across the street; blatant in their admiration.

Though I stood up, they remained a wall in front of me.

She had ripped the sleeves off her t-shirt, slashed it a couple times across the chest, so that her cleavage was revealed through two diagonal gashes; near parallel. The mini-skirt she was wearing was pulled up one thigh slightly.

The guys moved on and she was no longer on the corner. I scanned the other side of the street frantically, trying to spot her.

And there she was, tucked in by the entrance to a shabby car park, leaning against the wall, left foot up on the wall behind her, causing the hem of her skirt to ride up her thigh.

She swung her bag, all provocation and tease, blew bubbles with her gum. Her hair was all messed up, falling partly over her eyes while she looked up through the lids at passers-by.

Her head turned for a moment and she spotted me looking at her.

Blowing a kiss to me, she stepped out into the sunlight in front of a passing suit, talking to him, looking him in the eye, walking backwards at the same pace as he did forward, nodding every now and then, succeeding in getting him to stop before they reached the end of the block.

They talked for a minute or so. Then he nodded and headed around the corner. She looked at me, gave me the thumbs up, raised her eyebrows; *I told you so.* She began to follow him.

This was rapidly getting beyond the original joke I'd played. It had stopped being funny the moment she suckered that guy, made the deal, agreed to...

Just as she reached the corner, she turned to look at me, making sure I was looking and pulled at the rips in her t-shirt, revealing her nipple while her right hand lifted her skirt slightly, letting me see that she wasn't wearing any underwear.

And of course, this being New York, no-one but me saw this happen. Or if they did, they marked it down as just another ordinary freak in the city.

She turned the corner and was gone from my sight.

This had gone too far. My heart beating too hard. My breathing forced. I began to sprint after her.

I'd only been joking! She didn't need to score this point!

As I pushed through the group of guys who'd blocked my view earlier, I scattered them in all directions, a couple of them falling. I didn't have chance to see whether they were following me to seek retribution; in that moment, didn't care.

A taxi screeched to a halt as I ran into the street. If this had been uptown I'd have been dead but in Soho they sometimes went at a reasonable speed; streets too narrow for haste. I looked at the driver for a second but he was too busy cursing me and calming his passenger to take any notice.

I ran along the street, half expecting another car to hit me or one of the guys from the group to hit me; just waiting to be hit, period.

As I sprinted around the corner, tumbling around the edge of the building, Ivvy was standing there with the guy, both of them leaning against a wall, watching me. Waiting for me.

Smiling at the state of me, she turned to the man.

"There," she said, "I told you he would. Thanks so much for helping out."

He smiled back at her, offered his hand.

"It was nothing," he said with a heavy British accent, "glad to be of help."

He picked up his briefcase and walked up to me, stopping to speak.

"You're pathetic," he said, his words speckling my face with saliva, "sick!"

He regained his original direction, waved to Ivvy over his shoulder and was gone.

"What did you tell him?" I asked, still having trouble breathing.

She smiled at me but didn't say anything.

Eventually, my breath found its way back into my lungs.

"What did you say to him?"

Her grin turned lupine.

"That you're my boyfriend and you can't get it up unless I act like a hooker."

"Huh?"

"But if it looked like I'd actually made a deal, you'd be around that corner in a matter of seconds."

"What? Why did you do that?"

She stepped close to me. Flicked her fringe to get it out of the way. Looked me directly in the eye. Her voice hissed sibilance.

"Don't you ever pull that shit on me again, you hear me?"

We stared at each other for a long time as the city returned to its normal frenetic pace around us, destroying any hope of silence.

"You ripped your t-shirt," It was all I could think of to say.

She hooked her thumb in one of the slashes.

"Want another look?" she asked and her voice was barely concealed venom. The ice was thin beneath me.

"Margarita?" I asked.

She thought for a moment.

"Yup," she said, "right after you buy me another shirt."

We walked on without saying another word.

Chapter 11:
Family Rules – Part III

Jo heard the key in the front door and listened as Stuck-up and Trendy walked through to the living room. She hadn't realized until now how much she'd been anxious about their return.

"Hi," Trendy said.

Jo looked up from her copy of Cosmopolitan; an article about some place in Africa that she couldn't pronounce and an issue she didn't really care about, but at least it had passed the time.

Mentally, she finished the greeting: *How's he been?*

Baby Kenny had been asleep when she'd arrived earlier this evening, so she really hadn't had that much to do. As usual, they'd left pretty much as soon as she'd got there; itching to get out.

"Not a peep out of him," she said, tossing the magazine to one side.

Stuck-up and Trendy; labels she'd draped upon them over the past year of being Kenny's baby-sitter. Easy labels.

Trendy swayed slightly as he stood in the doorway.

It was true that she hadn't heard Kenny make a noise all night. As he was right at the other end of the landing from the stairs, from his parents' bedroom, from the rest of the house period, that wasn't so much of a surprise, though. Frankly, he could have been crying all night and she wouldn't have known.

If she'd been crap at her job.

But she was *good* at her job. So she'd checked on him every half an hour, popping her head around the door and listening.

Every thirty minutes.

Which was more than she thought *they* ever did.

Now they were here, Jo's anxiety had doubled. She shook slightly at the thought of making the suggestion. Despite the television, the Cosmopolitan, the regular checks on Ken, it had been at the back of her thoughts all evening.

Her conversation with Jamie. The click of two and two coming together.

Dare she suggest it? Really?

"Do you want a coffee?" Trendy slurred.

She checked her watch. A little after midnight. She was going to have to get a cab anyway, so what damage could a coffee do?

Besides, it gave her breathing space.

As if she needed more of that.

She nodded and followed Trendy to the kitchen, noticing how Stuck-up walked into the living room and picked up the discarded magazine. She tutted slightly as she placed it back neatly in the rack at the end of the sofa.

In the kitchen, Trendy swayed while he filled the kettle, swayed while he ground the beans, swayed while he prepared the cafétiere. Water gushed out of the kettle as he began to pour, scalding his hand and wrist.

All of a sudden he wasn't swaying any more.

"*Fuck!*" he yelled, dropping the kettle on the counter and spinning away from it. "*Fuck! Fuck! Fuck! Fuck!*"

All instinct and preparedness, Jo sped across the kitchen. Though he turned in panic, tumbling into her, her momentum pushed Trendy back towards the sink, where she opened the cold tap, reaching out calmly to grab his forearm and shove his wrist under the streaming water. He went to pull his arm away but she shushed him with all the experience gained from ten years' of baby-sitting and five years' professional nannying.

"Hold it under there until it goes numb," she said; voice of the catholic school, no debate.

He had begun to cry, so Jo held her arm around him while he waited for his hand to go numb. And even then, even with his skin reddening within the foaming jet of cold water, even in that moment of calm after the calamity, the suggestion still lurked, prodding at her, wanting to be spoken.

"I'll finish the coffees," Stuck-up said from behind them both, speaking for the first time since arriving home. She'd simply stood and watched the accident and, though Jo might have been inclined to put it down to drunkenness, she knew better. This one was a cold, cold fish.

Silence descended on the kitchen, punctuated by Trendy's sobs and Stuck-up refilling the kettle.

And in Jo's head, the suggestion, pushing like a contraction, wanting release, wanting out.

Eventually it was too much for her; the vacuum of the kitchen, sucking it right out of her before she could stop herself.

"I've got an idea," she said quietly.

Neither of them said anything.

Had she said even said it out loud? She'd been rehearsing the conversation so much over the past week that she might well have just begun to run it through in her head again.

She couldn't have said anything. Neither of them had even reacted.

She pulled his wrist out from under the water and looked at it. The scald was turning a nice shade of red.

"Have you got any Vaseline?" she asked.

"Huh?" he questioned, his eyes bleary with alcohol and tears. Across the kitchen, Stuck-up remained quiet.

"Some Vaseline, for the scald…"

"Oh," he shrugged and gestured at one of the cabinets, "in there, I think."

Jo walked over to the cabinet and opened it. It was full of all matter of bottles and jars, pills and ointments, bandages and boxes. The one thing she couldn't see, however, was petroleum jelly.

She began to root around in amongst the flotsam, trying to unearth her prize, digging and dredging. Suddenly, Stuck-up was beside her pushing her out of the way and reaching up into the cabinet, retrieving a medium tub of Vaseline almost immediately.

"Here," she said, shoving the jar forcefully into Jo's hands, "and I'll thank you not to physically assault my cabinets in the future."

Without another word, she turned her back on her husband and Jo and poured the coffee. Once the liquid was steaming in the mugs, she crossed to another cabinet and pulled out a sugar bowl, with a little silver spoon, which she placed alongside. That done, she walked out of the kitchen, down the hallway and up the stairs.

The lady had retired.

As Jo went to get the coffees, she heard Trendy tut behind her. And knew just how he felt.

She approached the kitchen table and he gestured to the other chairs.

"Sit down, why don't you?"

She went to do so but just before she sat, remembered the Vaseline across the kitchen, next to the kettle.

"Hang on a second."

Back at the table, she opened the jar and slathered a generous amount of the jelly on his scalded wrist. He winced as she did so, inhaling and exhaling in short bursts.

"There," she said, "we'll just put a bandage on that and you'll be fine. That was a pretty nasty burn..."

She found herself looking down the hallway, at the empty space his wife had left behind; the care she should have shown.

As Jo stood to find a bandage, Trendy stopped her with a simple question: "What was your idea?"

"Pardon?" she asked, anxiety flooding back into her as she turned back to face him.

"Your idea," he replied, "you said you'd had an idea?"

"Oh that," she said, thinking hard, "it's nothing. Not important, really."

He looked at her for a long moment, staring right in her eyes. She felt pinned against the cabinets like a butterfly under glass.

"We can bandage this later," he said, breaking the silence between them, "but for now, let's just talk, eh?"

This time he pointed at the chair opposite him.

"Sit," he said and she followed his instruction like a dog at obedience class.

She didn't know where to start. All that rehearsal and practice and turning it over and over and over until her head seemed to have turned upside down and now she just didn't know what to say to him. It had seemed such a simple thing when she'd been talking it through with Jamie. Such a simple thing.

"Well?"

"Ummmm..."

He dipped his head, raised his eyebrows, looked up at her, willing her to speak.

"Oh, come on," he said, "you've not gone all coy on me, surely?"

"Well," she took a long slug from her coffee, like she'd been crossing a desert for days.

He nodded at the cup. "You want something in that?"

After a moment's thought, she nodded. "Why not?"

He stood and walked out the kitchen, leaving her alone with her thoughts for a moment. Either he did it on purpose, giving her time to think, or it was just providence because by the time he returned with a bottle of single malt, she'd decided that this *was* the right time and that she *would* run the suggestion past him.

As he glugged scotch into her mug, she spoke, bringing a drunken smile to his face.

"Have I ever told you who my sister is?"

He thought for a moment and then shook his head.

"Thought not," she said.

"Anyone I know?" he asked, regaining his seat opposite her.

She nodded. "Jamie Masters."

He looked at her blankly for a second. "Jamie Masters," rolled the name around his mouth, closed his eyes, thought. "Jamie Masters, Jamie Masters, Jamie… Masters…"

She couldn't believe he hadn't heard of her. She was everywhere at the moment. On almost every newspaper and beginning to show up on television as well. He must have heard of her!

"Jamie Masters," he said finally, "it rings a bell but…"

Jo lent towards him, pouting a little and half-closing her eyes. He didn't seem to notice.

"Look at me," she said.

He did but there was no sign of his noticing her hint.

"Oh, Jesus! Do I have to spell it out?"

She fell back into her usual routine, undoing a couple of buttons at the top of her blouse and pulling the two sides apart until the bottom of her bra showed, her breasts curving up and out. She wasn't as buxom as Jamie but they were sisters and the same genes underpinned their size and shape. Though she couldn't have gone into the modelling game, Jo knew how to fill a bra. She pouted again, pushing her shoulders forward slightly, arching her back so that her cleavage tightened.

"Now do you get it?" she asked and was amazed to see the light-bulb click on, just as it always did when she aped her sister.

"No way!" he suddenly shouted. "Not that Jamie Masters? *The* Jamie Masters?"

She was used to this reaction, this incredulity; all because her sister showed her tits off in the tabloid press.

"Yes, that Jamie Masters," she said, buttoning her blouse and drinking from her coffee while he regained his composure.

"Wow!" he said when he'd got himself back under some measure of control. "But I don't get it; why tell me now?"

Now it came, all the preparation, the rehearsal, the practice, the turning over of angles and comments.

"She's going to have her own television show," Jo said quietly, "and they... Well, they..."

He was leaning forward, listening intently.

"They what?"

She sighed heavily.

"Well, you're both out so much and I have Ken most of the time and I... Well, I thought that..."

"What?"

"They need a baby on the show and Jamie thought that they could use Ken. She loves him."

Neither of them said anything for a long time.

Eventually, watching his face carefully, trying to read every emotion it held, Jo spoke.

"Probably a good thing Stuck-up went to bed, eh?"

He nodded, not even noticing the label.

"Fuck the coffee," he said, pulling the scotch bottle towards him and pulling out the cork, "I need a drink before we can talk about this."

Chapter 12:
To The Depths

She was on the street corner. Beyond her district; out of her depth.

This rich-bitch, slumming it, spending time in the ghetto.

And I was hurting. Needing. Wanting.

Shaking.

She had that look about her, an air of arrogance that only a pampered, preened princess could perpetuate. It was down to her eyes, the way she looked about herself; sneer of disgust shallow beneath her lipstick grin. Black dress, classic; chiffon wrap. Mid-heel shoes under which she would grind any poor sap who dared to look at her the wrong way, stabbing eyes with high-cost heels.

Beautiful, of course, fucking beautiful. Out of reach, out of this world.

In the alleyway alongside a deli, I shivered in the shadows.

The street was calm. Quiet. Like a sniper, like a landmine, like hidden memories.

Three weeks on the street, a week after the park, a week after I had dreamed a murder that really happened. His slashed throat, bloody and dripping; carousels twirling crimson. I hadn't reached the point of returning to my parents by then, although in my heart of hearts I knew it was close; I woke up thinking about it most days. The climb-down, the humble pie.

But on that evening, I still refused to go to them on bended knee, even though I had no money.

I had no money.

Which meant I had no fix. Which meant I was quaking in the alleyway, feeling the tremors vibrate through my arms and legs, deep within the core of the bones. My joints ached with premature arthritis, elbows and knees throbbing like toothache.

And she'd just wandered around the corner.

Like a billboard. Open for business.

Rich pickings.

What the hell was she doing down here? She had mid-town written all up and down. Hung all over her in couture and trinkets.

Rich pickings.

She looked up and down the street, seeking out something. A lover? A cab?

A black guy walked past the mouth of the alley, burgeoning afro held down by headphones, rap music chattering loud enough for me to hear from my nest of shadows. As he pulled level with the deli, he noticed her on the corner. His hands were at his ears within a second, ripping off his headphones and looping them round his neck, his hair springing back upright. He turned to her, made some gesture with his hand that I couldn't see.

"Daaamn, woman!" he shouted, "but ain't you fine?"

She ignored him, maintaining her gaze, staring up the street.

He took a step forward.

"Hey! You hear me?"

Still she blanked him.

He held both hands out, palms up in conciliation.

"Oh I'm sorry," he pleaded, "I'm not good enough to talk wit you? Am I too African for your fine bones?"

And now she turned on him, spearing him with a gaze that...

A childhood memory hit me so hard that I felt paralyzed for a moment.

Martin Sanderson sat on the floor, pinioned by that same look; Jamie.

The dust of the storeroom whirling about his shame.

The black guy, shot down, walked into the deli without another word; she headed in the other direction, similarly silent, towards the East River, the end of the street dark where open sky replaced foreground lights and crossing signs, Brooklyn beyond.

Me, trembling, hungry for some calm, shadowing her at twenty paces.

Wondering how I had come to this intention.

Knowing how I had come to this intention.

Unwilling to eat that humble pie just yet. No climb-down. Regardless of where my pride forced me to go.

* * *

"Well?"

Jamie looked at him. Looked through him.

For a moment, he found that words didn't want to come. More used to being the *bon vivant* at any party, recounting his youth and stories of unbridled passion, daring-do, chivalry and charm, this time Martin didn't know where to start.

He sat down on a large drum of scenery paint, rubbing his chin and sighing.

Jamie just stared at him. They had ten minutes until the next scene would be shot and she really needed to go to the toilet. She knew she shouldn't have agreed to meet him here. But he'd said it was important. That they *had* to talk. So she'd come. And now he was just sitting there.

She didn't have time for his theatrics. None of them did.

They were all tired from years of pandering to his ageing sensitivity; creeping senility. Five long years.

"Oh, for fuck's sake, Martin, will you just spit it out!"

"I think we should ask for more money," he whispered.

"What?"

"A raise," he looked at her now, or at least in her direction, still not meeting her eyes, "we all deserve it."

No we don't, she thought, recalling her agent's advice, *I'm the star of this show and I'm getting a pretty good deal already. You're the one who's so drunk most of the time that he doesn't know how to negotiate a reliable contract. Or can't get an agent interested enough to take care of it in the meantime.*

She also knew it wasn't what he'd wanted to say.

"Is that what you asked me here for?" she scoffed, "a conversation about your rate of pay? Why don't you ask me about the bloody weather while you're at it? Is that what you wanted me here for?"

He looked back at the floor and shook his head.

No, she thought, *it bloody well isn't, is it?*

Because she knew exactly what he wanted.

Exactly.

And she wanted to rub the salt deep into his wounds. Beyond compassion. Far beyond.

She took a couple of steps towards him and touched the tips of her fingers beneath his chin, tilting his head up until it was level with her chest.

"Is it these?" she asked, knowing the answer already, playing her own game now, "the other night?"

Tears had begun to form in the corners of his eyes.

He nodded.

"You still want to touch them?"

He nodded again, a single drop of water running down his cheek.

"To stroke them?"

Gratitude flirted with his mouth, twisting it into a grimace she tried to ignore.

"To touch me?" she continued.

Her other hand came up from her side and she began to stroke upward from her left hip, towards her breast. His eyes followed its movement; hypnotized.

"Like this?"

He nodded frantically.

She licked her lips hard enough to make sure he would be able to hear it. Leant towards him slightly, so that her perfume could fill the space between them.

Remembering the touch of his hands on her at the party, the fun of flirting, of kissing and knowing it was going no further, of feeling his old man's erection through the material of his trousers, pressing against her hip while he tried to remember what it was to be a young teenager again. His tweed trousers and button down shirt.

Remembered telling him: *"Be patient, take your time."*

Remembered breathing in his face, Bacardi and Coke vaporising between them, overcoming the waves of scotch coming off him.

Remembered telling him: *"Maybe later tonight, eh?"*

And then leaving the party as soon as she could find her coat.

"Oh Jamie," he said now on a breath, moving a little; paint can rattling on the cement floor of the storeroom.

Her hand continued its meandering journey up her ribs, counting them one by one with her first two fingers. Sanderson counting along with her, transfixed.

Her thumb brushed the underside of her breast and she sighed slightly, lips parting, tongue wetting them again.

"Is that good?" she asked him, *"is it?"*

He nodded.

"Yes."

"It feels good," she continued, voice getting quieter, almost whispering, "it's really good. Really…"

Her hand moved over the swell and she squeezed slightly, crumpling the material of her t-shirt.

"Oh," she sighed.

"Yes," he echoed.

Her right hand moved so quickly that it surprised them both, grabbing his chin and pulling it upwards, his neck cracking as the whiplash hit him.

Her left hand flew, slapping him hard across his cheek.

"You filthy, disgusting pervert!" Jamie yelled. *"Where the fuck do you get off trying it on with me? Eh?"*

She shoved him backwards and he tumbled off the can.

Neither of them noticed the door opening.

Sanderson landed in a heap, clattering into brooms and mops stacked in the corner. Dust whirled up about his head.

Jamie just stood, staring down at him, content in her ruse, her success in humiliating him.

He was pathetic.

Old. Past it. Drunk.

Pathetic.

"Jamie? What's happening?" Kenny asked from just behind her left shoulder.

She didn't even turn to look at him where he stood in the doorway, the bright lights of the corridor forming a halo around his little boy's silhouette.

"Nothing Kenny," she said, "nothing for you to worry about."

"But…"

"But *nothing*, Kenny. All right?"

She sensed him taking a step forward. Out of the corner of her eye she could see him now, looking up at her, looking down at Martin, his almost comical double take, his five year old brain trying to make sense of the scene being played out amidst bottles of bleach and scouring powder. Still she stared the old fart down.

"Martin?" Kenny tried an alternative approach.

But the old man said not a word in reply, nor twitched a muscle.

Kenny stared up at Jamie for a moment, rooted to the spot.

"Leave, Kenny," she finally said, "just go. And shut the door behind you."

He paused for a moment, looked from one to the other one final time, turned and walked out of the room.

He followed orders and made sure the door closed behind him.

*   *   *

She looked out at the East River.

And I was sure that she was playing some movie in her head, watching herself from distance, camera panning in to highlight her elegance; her untapped emotions, just waiting for the right man to unlock her core.

How else could she possibly have explained being down here at this time of night? In this area. And seemingly so oblivious to the danger all around her.

I made it quick, hitting her from behind. Smashing her head against the railing enough to disorient her, ripping the chain of pearls from round her neck, the bracelet from her wrist, the purse from under her arm.

Running before I had chance to think.

She was screaming as she realised what had happened.

But there was no-one there to help her. She should have known that before she ventured that far into the dark side of town; before the cameras rolled.

She screamed for help.

I ran, pocketing my gains, hoping they would be enough to trade for a little hit.

Ripping open the purse as I ran, rifling through to the cash that I knew she'd have in there somewhere. No interest in the cards. No need for them. I just needed a little fix. A little something to keep me warm on this May night.

She had about fifty bucks in there.

So I didn't even need to worry about the pearls and bracelet.

I retrieved them from my pocket and dropped them immediately, throwing the purse alongside. Pocketing the fifty, I slowed to a walk.

And even though the exercise and adrenalin had made the aching and trembling ten times worse, I knew they would soon be gone. I felt good.

Good enough to forget what I'd done.

What I'd come to.

What had I come to?

Chapter 13:
Memories Fade

I looked at him as he sat reading his *Wall Street Journal*. One leg crossed over the other, foot tapping slightly, always agitated, always focused on the next action, the next task to hit his *'to do'* list.

He had a PDA by then that beeped at him when he was overdue.

Sometimes I couldn't stand to be in the same room as him, as either of them, especially when they were together. Which wasn't very often. Not by then.

I couldn't tell you how old my father is.

I know his birthday, October twenty-third. Don't know what year.

Not all information sticks.

I was in my early twenties. He looked to be in his fifties.

A gulf between us.

Not all information sticks in my head.

Though some things stick in my throat.

* * *

I have one memory of him that recurs.

One memory. Hardly a testament to a life well lived; a relationship well loved.

In this memory, my father tickles me.

I must have been more than three because I remember being able to talk to him about it at the time. Laugh about it, joke about it.

Friday evenings.

When he'd been starting his career in advertising, a junior project manager or whatever it was he'd been doing, he would always manage to get home early on Fridays. All my filming was done by then, so I would generally be home by Friday lunchtime, spending time with my Nanny, or an au pair, or whoever else they'd hired to keep me company. Until four-thirty came around.

At which time, I would be laying flat on my back in the middle of the lounge, legs stretched flat on the floor, arms out in a crucifix. Me, a little Jesus pinned to the living room rug.

Because my father was coming home early.

Because my father would tickle me just as soon as he walked through the door.

There I lay, every Friday afternoon, waiting for my father to come home from work, spread-eagled on the carpet for the pleasure of his laugh; his love.

The first time he didn't show, I laid there until seven p.m. The au pair tried her best but I was a rock; steadfast, resolute. Stubborn.

I don't know how long it took, how many weeks of him not arriving when I expected, but eventually I was there in the middle of the lounge for only ten minutes or so. In memory, retrospective blurring of time, it feels like only another moment or two before four-thirty on a Friday afternoon came and went without any activity on my part, save the slight twinge of something – too young for it to be melancholia or sadness or regret or remorse or loss or any other of those analysis words that I've learnt to lay over it in the intervening years.

It's one of the few memories I have of my father from when I was growing up and it shines in, and because of, its isolation. I wish I could say it has the warm glow of tenderness but mostly the memory is of the tickles going away, of the emptiness of those Friday afternoons when he'd gone to some bar in Fleet Street rather than come home to play with his son, choosing to have a drink or two with the trendy media fuck-ups who could help further his career.

That's my memory.

Desertion.

Chapter 14:
A New Addiction

I stole over twenty cars in the three years after the dead man in Washington Square. Since I had first felt the adrenalin rush of playing cat and mouse with the police.

Since the birth of my new addiction.

I kept count on my bed frame, where the headboard was attached to its post. The marks were small but enough for me to know that they were there. Sometimes, I ran my fingers over them when I couldn't sleep; autohypnosis, my own version of counting sheep.

*   *   *

The first time I jacked a car, it was on the spur of the moment. I'd long since stopped stealing for my habit; long since waved goodbye to anything that I couldn't buy from the money they left for me every month.

But the rush of the stealing, that stayed with me. The street-sleeper's clothes, the murder in Washington Square, the socialite choosing to slum it, all the others who have come and gone along that dangerous path; pure adrenalin and the fear of getting caught.

Impossible to give away for good.

So when I was walking down forty-second towards the UN building, towering over the East River, and I came across a beat up old Chevy parked outside a hotel, engine running, no sign of its owner, I was in the driver's seat before I could think about it. Gunning the engine, heading off up the street, cresting a rise towards First, spotting the running driver as a speck in my rear-view before asphalt cut him off behind me. From the UN, I dropped onto the FDR around the south of the island, crossing from lane to lane but not really pushing the speed limit, still wondering what the hell I was doing, expecting the police to appear in my rear-view at any moment, waving at me to pull over, sirens blaring, lights strobing, blinding me until I had no choice but to concede the chase. I got as far as the Hudson parkway at Seventy-ninth, where I pulled over by the basketball courts, leaving the keys in the car and walking away; letting someone else steal it from there, letting them get caught.

I was shaking with the thrill of it, the purity of the rush.

And all the time, careening through my head: *what the fuck are you doing?*

Since then, it had been a near-regular occurrence. Almost but not quite enough to establish a pattern by which anyone could track me.

Paranoia is a great thing when it comes to protecting yourself.

Manhattan was not a good place to steal cars. Too many stop lights, too many people, too much traffic. After the fifth car, anxiety began to kick in. Manhattan may have been a waste of time but New Jersey? That was a different thing all together.

New Jersey.

So close over the river, so ripe for the picking.

No-one in their right mind left Manhattan to steal a car in New Jersey. All attention was on crime travelling in the opposite direction.

Which is why I started crossing the Hudson out to New Jersey.

It was more difficult to spot idling cars outside of the city, of course. Much more difficult. The average Jersey Joe didn't pull up and leave the engine running while he picked up some smokes or a bottle of booze.

Didn't stop me trying, though.

Once I got to my tenth car, a PT Cruiser, I'd worked out a pretty healthy rhythm.

Gas stations. Near freeways.

I started checking traffic reports after sitting for forty minutes at the George Washington Bridge, watching traffic queued with no movement, weighing up whether it was worth making a dash through the E-ZPass lane, knowing that the cars were just as blocked on the far side, knowing that no matter what I did, I was in a stolen car. Better to get out and run. Which is what I did. Hoping no-one would remember enough about me to relay to the police. I couldn't even cross the bridge on foot; too easy for them to get me at either end. Like I say, paranoia is a great defence mechanism. I walked for miles before heading back to Manhattan; chalking it up to experience.

Once I got into my flow, though, I found it took less than an hour to spot the idiot who left their keys in the car while they went into the gas station, many of which were pre-pay by this time. There was always one who went back in to buy a little something extra or use the bathroom.

Then I'd swoop; in the car, out of the lot before anyone had chance to notice.

It all came down to the experience, the planning.

Never pick a car that's expensive enough to have satellite tracking.

Realised that after the fourth one.

Counted my luck once more.

I started to think about gas station close-circuit monitors after the seventh.

And about police reports after the ninth; fantasies of televised chases filmed by the cameras concealed under the hoods of pursuit cars.

Police are seeking a Caucasian male, mid-twenties, who waits until drivers enter the gas station before stealing the unlocked car, keys in the ignition...

It all began to play through my mind.

I scattered my net wide, kept a list of where I'd been, hidden under my mattress; incriminating evidence should I ever be caught.

Eventually I decided to adopt a disguise of sort; cloaking myself in this country's barely concealed prejudice.

I had Ivvy to thank for the idea; though she had no idea about my new addiction.

One night at her apartment, she'd been drunk and posturing about society and all its ills, quoting from *Bowling For Columbine* that the media fed America images of black men as criminals and set a stereotype that rap reinforced to the point of self-fulfilling prophecy. So that when people saw black they thought criminal.

So the next time I went to Jersey, I dressed in hip-hop gear, black hat, jacket and trousers, basketball vest underneath, adopting a walk that no white boy has ever learnt to perfect. I chose sunglasses at night. Dim lots; shadows doing my work.

Enough of a stereotype for the camera; grainy evidence of surveillance television.

If the police were looking for anyone, it was a black guy who stole cars from isolated Jersey gas stations while the driver went back in after filling up.

Like they'd pay any attention to that.

My new addiction.

And, boy, was I addicted.

Chapter 15:
Family Rules - Part IV

The set-up was quite simple.

Jamie Masters as the young mother, one-year-old kid, live-in boyfriend, mother who didn't really like either of them but doted on her grandchild and the boyfriend's father, forced to move in after his house was destroyed in a fire. Put them all together in a small two-up-two-down and hilarity would ensue. Couldn't be easier. The BBC would be disappointed to learn that they'd turned it down at an earlier pitch.

But Thames picked it up and ran with the ball.

On the basis of its being a vehicle for Jamie, of course. Which is why they named her character after her; the norm in America but not so in the UK.

They might as well have called it *Jamie Saves The Day!* Because that's what she did week in week out, as her boyfriend kept promising to deal with his father. Who was rapidly becoming the object of Jamie's mother's affection; a bad thing, as he had a crush on Jamie, worshipped the ground she walked on, mobilised against his own son at every twist and turn.

And though it sounded complicated in synopsis, it worked like a dream on screen.

Besides, it was nothing compared to the off-screen dramas that underpinned the performance. And kept the public hooked to both story-lines.

In the first two series, Ken was little more than a prop, seemingly subtitled whenever he was on screen.

Here, the baby in Jamie's arms: *Jamie is a caring mother.*

Here, her boyfriend tries to change the baby's nappy with hilarious results: *He can't care for the baby as well as Jamie (he needs Jamie).*

The old man bends over the cot: *Oh no! What's he going to do this time?*

Subtly hidden by camera angles, Jamie breast-feeds the baby: *Bet you wish it was you, don't you lads?*

They all grimace: The baby's stunk out the room again!

They might as well have used a toy doll.

For the first two series, they could have replaced him with moulded plastic.

Until he learnt to talk.

Then, all bets were off.

Because over the course of the next three years, slowly, quietly and effortlessly, Ken went about the business of stealing the show.

Chapter 16:
A Darkening Sky

We sat in Central Park watching the sun descend into smog and calamitous traffic, dipping behind the trees that rim Sheep Meadow; Ivvy and I high as kites, fluttering in the breeze, flitting from idea to idea, laughing at each other, with each other.

It was our anniversary. A year previously, I had been walking through Washington Square when this blonde woman asked if I was carrying. Every day of that year had been interminable, every hour had witnessed a gut-wrenching wrestling match between the twin poles of my pinball life: the needle, my parents. Matter and anti-matter; addiction and anti-addiction, magnetism and repulsion.

We go together 'cos opposites attract...

"What was that?" Ivvy asked, looking at me.

"Huh?"

She snorted laughter.

"What?"

"You sang something. Just then."

"Did I?"

"Yeah, sounded like and old Janet Jackson song or something like that."

"Oh," I nodded as if I understood what she was on about but didn't say anything else. I stared at space, stared at trees, stared at the sun disappearing behind the buildings of the Upper West Side.

Ivvy's hand snaked into mine and she leant her head on my shoulder.

I stared at the New York sunset. Taxis blared over on Fifth; smell of horseshit from carriages that circle the park all day.

Up to that moment, Ivvy had never shown much in the way of affection toward me; none other than junkie solidarity.

"Mmmmm..." She snuggled against my shoulder.

And I was close to crumbling, biting back the words.

I don't know what to do.

I don't know what to do.

I don't know what to do.

*   *   *

"One day, Kenny, you won't be saying that," Sanderson winked at him.

"I will," the boy implored.

"Trust me," the old man winked, "you won't. What do you think, Jamie?"

Sitting over the other side of the set, flicking through a magazine, Jamie looked up at the little boy and old fruit, conspiring in the make-believe dining room.

"What do I think about what?" she asked.

"Kenny here says that he won't ever have a girlfriend."

"Ever," Kenny added, just to make sure.

Jamie smiled at him, her face pure indulgence. All of them loved that little boy, more so every day. In the same glance, she couldn't help but notice how Sanderson leered back at her; subconscious response. She turned away, ignoring him as best she could. She'd had three years of his lasciviousness, his barely concealed lust, all the time coming ever closer to speaking with Joel about it, making a scene, getting the director to deal with it, calling in some of the favours she was owed for making this the huge series it had become.

For now, though, she sought escape in turning her attention back to Kenny, his blue eyes, his cherubic nose, angelic smile.

"Sorry," she said, smiling, " it ain't gonna happen like that, love."

He frowned in response, flushing slightly.

"Seriously," Jamie added, nodding down at herself, "one day, you're gonna love these things."

"Eurgh," Ken replied.

"She's right, lad," Sanderson chimed in, "you will love them."

"Unless you're queer like that old poof," Jamie sniggered to see Sanderson's face at this; his carefully protected, projected masculinity.

"What's queer?" Kenny asked of his screen-family, even giving a little shrug, palms-up, raising his eyebrows with the question.

"That," Joel said as he walked on set, appearing from the direction of the edit suite, "is enough of that. Time enough to learn the birds and the bees when you go to big school. Right now, we've got a fucking show to put together, all right?"

Jamie and Sanderson looked at each other, suddenly in collusive world-weary solidarity at the director's habitual bad mood.

Joel had only grown worse over the years.

Jamie stood, dropping the magazine back where it had been left by the set designer; all belongings seemed to be props these days. As she did so, she broke eye contact with Sanderson.

The old man chose to watch her stand, staring at the way her various curves pressed at her clothing, watching the way her nipples made slight peaks against the material of her t-shirt, staring until he feared that to walk would be to admit his lust all too obviously.

"Come on then Kenny, my beautiful boy," Jamie said, walking over to him and putting her arm around his shoulders, giving his head a little rub. As they walked off set, she called back over her shoulder.

"Are you coming, Martin?"

"Not... Er... Not just yet," he replied, voice on the verge of breaking, throat too dry.

He sat.

Sat in his chair until his untimely erection had faded.

*　　*　　*

I pulled my shoulder out from under her head and she fell against me slightly.

"Ow! What did you do that for?" Ivvy asked.

"Well, you..."

"I what?"

"You..."

"You asshole! What did you have to go and do that for? It was nice, you know, lying here with you and watching the sun go down and then you have to go and do something like that. You asshole! *You fucking asshole!*"

Her mouth running a mile a minute.

And she was right, it had been nice. But it had also been... What? Threatening? Was that it? No, not exactly. But I'd been shaking. I tried to explain.

"Ivvy, I..."

But she'd turned to face me and now lunged forward, pushing me backwards onto the grass, her face huge as her mouth clamped over mine, her jaw working, tongue darting into my mouth, breath tasting of coffee and she was heavy against me and hot and the day was ending and the stench of horseshit pervaded everything and her tongue was licking the back of my teeth and I wanted to breathe, I really wanted to breathe, all I wanted to do was breathe, I really wanted to…

I pushed against her, so that she rolled back and away from me, disappearing from sight momentarily. I stared at the darkening sky overhead and took in a huge, whooping breath

She didn't move.

I didn't move.

Neither of us said anything for an age.

Finally, I heard her voice, almost a whisper.

"Sorry," she said, "I shouldn't have. Shouldn't…"

"Don't worry, you couldn't help yourself."

She sat up.

"What?"

I shook my head, unsure of what I'd even said.

"*I couldn't help myself?* Did you really just say that?"

She stood up, towering over me.

I shook my head again.

She picked up her bag, rummaging around in it until she found a hairbrush to drag through her dirty blonde raffia hair while she searched for the right words.

"I'm going home," she said, "are you coming?"

I thought for a moment and then nodded, lifting my hand up so that she could help me to my feet.

"Yeah, right!" she derided and started walking south, leaving me on my backside surrounded by grass and horseshit stench.

"Ivvy!" I shouted, getting to my feet. *"Wait for me!"*

She didn't.

I ran to catch up.

Chapter 17:
Claustrophobia And
The Mirror

Ivvy had got hold of this book from somewhere: *The Earth from the Air.*

We'd spent most of an evening poring over the pages, diving into the most amazing photos. When we'd first flicked through them, they looked like postcards or pieces of fabric. Nothing special.

Like one of them, a jagged stripe of orange against a black background, modern art at best; simple, inconsequential concept. Then, looking closer, there's a small plane flying above the orange stripe and I'd found myself thinking: *no way... that can't be...* And I'd realize over and again that these were pictures of the Earth. Of people. Of nature. These tiny, tiny pictures of enormous, breathtaking scale.

We sat on the couch, getting high, looking at the pictures, falling ever more deep in their thrall.

"Can you believe this?" Ivvy said and pointed at a shepherd and his goats, clustered within a rickety fence. From where I was sitting it looked like dried grass piled up ready to burn in the midday sun.

"Wow!"

"Understatement…"

I looked at her, she smiled.

We were quiet together for a moment, taking a hit off our shared joint, pausing, snickering smoke out into the room.

"Jesus!"

She was back to flicking through the pictures.

"Huh?"

She pointed at a grid of multi-coloured squares in the book.

"Mondrian, right?"

Lazy days wasting time in the Guggenheim, an education through avoidance.

Ivvy shook her head.

"Dye pits in Iran," she explained, patient as a toad, "you don't know how it works yet?"

I smiled, a little laugh escaping me. "Maybe…" I said, "and then again, maybe I don't want to know how it works. Maybe I'm just playing with you."

She stared at me. Smiled. Stuck up the middle finger of her left hand.

We both erupted dope sniggers.

"It wouldn't work if it was the world," I said when we were back to breathing normally, making no sense, not even to myself.

"Huh?" She was flicking through the pages.

"If it was the world. You know… those pictures where they show whole cities as smudges on the globe. You know? The lights at night, the roads in-between just dotted lines. You know what I mean? Right?"

Ivvy looked at me. Didn't nod or shake her head.

"Right?" I repeated, certain that she was just playing me.

She slapped the book shut and tossed it onto the couch between us. It was heavy enough to make me bounce a little.

"Whatchoo talkin' 'bout, Willis?" she said, frowning, and we were both laughing again before we could stop ourselves.

"When I luh... look..." I started but the giggles were in the way, choking my words. And suddenly, taking me by surprise, a knot in my throat, my laughter in danger of turning to sobs.

I grabbed my beer and drank heavily, almost gagging as bubbles rushed up the back of my throat, into my nose.

"There's... enough to care about," I said, staring at my beer bottle, "you can see enough. If they were more distant... It would be easy to, you know, just take a glance and move on. But there's something about them that makes them... me..."

I couldn't say another word.

Not one word.

She grabbed the bottle from my hand, drained it, threw it down by the side of the couch at her end.

"Ken," she said, taking my hand, "what the fuck is up with you?"

"I... I don't know... I just..."

She squeezed my hand.

How could I tell her? How could I tell her that when I looked at those pictures, at the depth of them, at the little people and animals and cars and houses and farms and planes and all the other collected shit, I could almost taste the lives, almost know what each and every one of them went through every day? How could I tell her that? How could I tell her that looking at those pictures just brought the reality of my shitty little life crashing home like a punch to my stomach; the empty, barren plains between wherever I was and wherever my parents wished I would be? That when I looked at those pictures I could almost smell wherever they were taken, Iran, China, England, Arizona, New York, wherever? How could I tell her that the pictures made me feel smaller than a mosquito and just as easily smacked into oblivion?

How could I tell her that it didn't matter where I went?

Because no matter how far away I might believe I'd escaped, no matter where I might run, the truth was that *I* would still be there. No matter where I went, I could never get away from who I am.

The pit of my stomach roiled with these thoughts. I felt like puking.

The pictures made me think of my father.

For no reason. No cause for this effect.

Just my father.

How could I tell her all this and not sound like I was tripping?

Ivvy. I wanted to trust her. I wanted to tell her all this shit.

But I couldn't.

I stood up.

"Where are you going?" she asked, voice hardening, confused, losing its warmth.

"I can't," I said and headed towards the door. I heard her behind me, following, throwing things out of her way; she kicked over her glass, a chair rattling on the wooden floor as she threw a cushion at it.

"Just you wait a fucking minute!" Ivvy yelled but I was moving.

The door was open and I was out, heading down the stairs. Three flights and I would be out into New York's oblivion.

Behind me, I heard her again.

"Fuck!" she yelled, "not the great, disappearing Ken show again!"

I kept walking.

And heard her on the landing above me.

Kept walking.

Heard her scream: *"WELL FUCK YOU, YOU ASSHOLE! DON'T COME AROUND NO MORE, I WON'T BE HOME!"*

Kept walking.

Down the stairs; resolute and steady.

Needing a hit.

The buzz.

One little rush of adrenalin and the chase.

Of risk.

Of fear.

Of success.

One little hit.

Even before I got to the street, I knew that I was heading to New Jersey.

To steal a car from a gas station.

While the owner was inside buying a soda or a doughnut or a strip of beef jerky or a lottery ticket or whatever other shit people buy at gas stations.

I hopped on a bus to Port Authority.

From there to my fix. Over the river.

Jersey.

Chapter 18: Oblivion

The first time I used heroin was about three weeks before my eighteenth birthday. That conscious decision, aping Cobain – a single, self-destructive streak that threatened to pull me down whenever I get too sober; too aware of reality. I scored from an old high-school friend I knew was into that sort of shit, history of truancy, hanging with a gang, all of it. Ten bucks. My first taste. Ten bucks.

I melted.

My eighteenth was a blur, with me floating through the whole thing.

Eighteen.

And feeling like I was five again.

* * *

I'd been lying there for over half an hour.

"Kenny... Ken... Kenneth?"

My father's voice.

"Is he breathing?" she asked from behind him.

"Oh shut up," his voice exasperated but holding a note of panic that was unusual, normally so calm, so collected, so *not* worried about his son, "of course he's breathing."

"Have you checked?" She was persistent, demanding.

My mother, born with a silver spoon in her mouth and a demand on her lips.

"No, I haven't bloody well checked, you stupid cow! I don't need to, I can see he's..."

"Have you checked?" She was firm.

There was something about her voice. Something.

"All right!" his voice faded as he crossed the room, away from me. "I'll check he's breathing, all right? Will that make you happy?"

His voice getting louder as he came back, stomping noise of his feet on the wood flooring of the apartment.

"Go on son, breathe," he ordered but I didn't do anything different, just lay there listening to them.

Which was difficult because they chose to be silent for a moment or two.

If I could have remembered how to open my eyelids, I would have. I honestly would.

"Well?" she started to ask.

"Nothing," he said quietly, finally.

"Nothing?" That something in her question.

"Nothing."

There was a moment of calm, of complete and utter certainty.

Then she screamed.

And screamed.

And screamed.

But didn't come any nearer to me.

Never near to me, never.

I caught the odd word, the odd phrase, what they should do, where they should go, who they should call, how did this happen, all the shit that came flying from her mouth.

Her externalized thought careened around the room; at the calm centre, I remained, untouched by the hurricane.

"Shut up," he said, quietly.

She didn't comply with his order.

"Shut up," his voice more forceful this time, slightly louder.

No response.

I opened my eyelids a fraction, viewing them through blurred lashes.

He slapped her straight across the face, her head rocking back with the force of the blow. I lay still, trying to make sense of what I was seeing.

She fell silent, shocked, staring at him. Her hand lifted to the red mark developing on her cheek.

He raised his other hand; a mirror.

"I was joking," he said, waving the reflective surface at her. It caught the sunlight falling through the window and caused it to dance around her eyes.

"You were…"

He nodded in response.

"You are so bloody stupid," he chided, "that sort of thing only works in the movies. Don't you know anything?"

She didn't say anything, just stared at him.

And stared at him.

I watched this, not daring to move.

He threw the mirror onto the chest-of-drawers and turned to walk out of the room.

She let him get through the door before shouting after him.

"Wait! Where do you think you're going?"

"I need a drink," he replied without altering his stride.

"A drink?" she yelled, *"how can you think about drinking when..."*

She glanced in my direction, not long enough to notice I was watching.

Now he stopped, turned around, came back into the bedroom, coming towards the bed.

I closed my eyes.

And he was scooping me up onto his shoulders, his broad shoulders, turning back toward the door.

"Right," he replied through closed teeth, "I'll just get him to the hospital, shall I? Tell them that our little boy has gone to sleep and we really don't have an idea what to do because we're so bloody stuck-up that we would never be expected to look after our own children, would we? It's up to the bloody nanny to know what to do if ever there's an emergency... Are you coming with me?"

She didn't reply and he decided to twist the dagger a little.

"Oh come on, not against going to the hospital are you? Not afraid that you might catch some infection from the dreadfully poor people who frequent that nasty, *dirty* place, are you?"

His voice dripped sarcasm. He had spoken the something; her voice filled not with anxiety but instead the risk of embarrassment at being uncovered as an uncaring parent. The fear of being found out, seething within her.

"There's..." her voice was tiny, as if mumbling to herself, "there's no need to be like that. I... I didn't know what to..."

"No, you bloody well didn't, did you?"

"I..."

"Should have thought."

"No, I…"

"Should have thought before screaming blue murder and getting me to race halfway across London just to check whether my six-year old son was dead or not?"

"No, I'm…"

"A waste of space? Better at doing Harvey-Nicholls than being a parent?"

"That's not fair," she said, voice hardening back to its more usual steel in chiffon, "not at all."

"True though, isn't it?"

"I was about to apologise," her voice hardening, "but you're too much of a prick to deserve it."

She pushed past him as she left the room, hitting him hard enough to set him off balance. He span, tumbling backwards onto the bed. I bounced from his shoulder, landing on the pillows. Though I tried to fight it back, there was nothing I could do; I started to laugh.

"Huh?"

I couldn't keep the giggles back.

"Kenny?"

I laughed.

"Oh, you little bastard!"

Though his words spoke of anger, his voice was mellowing; relief coming through.

"I was…" I spoke through gasps for air, "just… pretending… I…"

He slapped me so hard I fell off the bed.

Walked out the room.

Slammed the door behind him.

I sat there, beginning to cry.

I cried until I fell asleep on the floor.

Where I woke up the next day.

Chapter 19:
In Plain Sight

At Port Authority, I changed into my costume, my hip-hop cloak of invisibility. I didn't skulk in the corner or find a quiet sidewalk, I got changed in amongst the throngs of passengers coming and going along the ground floor concourse, timing my changes to the beat patterns of the cops.

The way I'd always figured it, I was safe in the one over-riding quality of the big city, the commonality of *"if I ignore it it'll go away"*. These were people who could walk past someone getting mugged, someone screaming rape, someone shooting up in a main-street doorway and later say that they hadn't seen anything.

Gee, officer, I didn't even hear him speak to me... Wow... That really happened while I was... Wow...

Over in the corner there was a young lad sitting on a back-pack. He was wearing combats and a blue shirt, short-sleeved, paisley whorls all over the material; back against the wall at the side of a small news-stand, the other wall at his left side, leaving only his right flank open to the public. When I'd first glanced, I thought he might be rolling a joint, or checking the stuff he'd picked from someone's pocket but as I watched him, I realised that his being wedged into the corner was more an act of protection. It was in the way he looked about himself, his eyes a little wild, checking every person who came within fifteen feet of his makeshift island.

A little while earlier when NYPD's finest walked past, the boy had looked up with the most amazing smile of thanks on his face.

Definitely a tourist; this young teenage boy away from home for the first time, scared shitless by the seething mass of humanity that was Port Authority at rush hour. He needed some help, some support.

I could have walked over there, bent down to speak to him, shown my empty palms to reassure him I was no threat, finding out whether he was lost, whether he was waiting for someone, or if it was just a case of a gypsy cab driver picking him up at the airport and ripping him off for all the money he had.

I could have done that.

But I had my own craving to fix and my bus was scheduled to leave in ten minutes. I had to become my black alter ego and get to the gate. I began to change there on the concourse; a couple of minutes until the cop came back around again.

The boy watched me. Every so often, I glanced in his direction and found him staring at me, eyes ever wider.

I could read the thoughts driving the expression on this face.

That guy is getting changed here and now in front of me and nobody fucking well seems to care! None of them!

Here was this terrified boy, alone in the madness, silent in the crowd, staring at a skinny white guy pulling on a bag-load of hip hop gear, topping it off with a woollen cap even though for most of the day the city had roasted in the high eighties. A terrified boy that I didn't have time nor inclination to care about.

I had a bus to catch; a bus to my one remaining high, adrenalin. I started towards the gates.

A woman walked up to the boy.

He stared at her knees for what felt like an age, not wanting to meet her eyes, hoping she would go away, leave him alone to his burgeoning panic. But she was going nowhere. She crouched, said something, and his head snapped up to look at her. Recognition flared, shattering his fear, smearing relief across every curve of his smiling face. He lunged forward, grabbed her around the neck and hugged her tight.

Which made me think of Ivvy in the park that time, the one time she'd kissed me, when I acted like an asshole and destroyed most of the trust we'd built up over that whole long year of joints and smack and speed and acid and every other chemical we'd forced upon our quaking physiology.

I carried on past the boy and his rescuer, ever more eager to be on that bus, heading to Jersey, to the one thing that now gave my life any purpose.

*   *   *

As the bus pulled out of Port Authority, heading down the ramp and into the network of slipways that enter the Lincoln Tunnel, I was thinking of my parents.

Off in Europe, their departing message that terse, unfeeling note from my father. I knew better than to try to read something more into it than what it said.

My father didn't care for me very much more than my cold, cold mother. Even then, that caring was little more than a way to make his life run as smoothly as possible.

For many years, he'd chosen to lose himself in work, an easy task given the headiness of the eighties, the down of the early nineties, the resurgence of the dot-com bubble. My father surfed those waves with a vigour that was inversely proportional to his desire to spend any time with me.

My parents, as foreign to me as Outer Mongolia.

Over in Europe now, doing the family thing, burying a grandfather I hardly knew.

I didn't wish them well in their travels.

All I cared about was that, for a little while, the apartment was mine. And given the way things had been between Ivvy and I, that wasn't such a bad thing.

The bus rumbled into the maw of the Lincoln tunnel, its roar amplified by reflection from the tunnel's tarnished tiles, all cacophony and sonics; harmonics and sub-bass.

I leaned my head on the window to feel the thrum of the bus, feeling the vibration, something akin to life.

I woke up as soon as the bus pulled to its first stop amidst the pseudo-Manhattan that had grown on the other side of the Hudson.

Wide awake.

Adrenalised. Ready for the chase.

Ready for the takedown.

Chapter 20:
Family Rules – Part V

"It's really quite simple," the doctor said, closing his notes, leaning forward in his chair slightly, adding emphasis, gaining gravitas.

"Your son is suffering from depression. I hesitate to label him manic at this stage, a little early considering his... Ah... Young age, however the situation should be monitored. Definitely of concern."

"Depressed? How..."

"I hope you appreciate just what your son has been through in the past six years?"

"Appreciate?"

The psychologist formed a steeple of fingers beneath his chin; stared Ken's father in the eyes for a moment.

"How old are you?"

"Huh?"

"Your age. How old are you?"

"I'm thirty-nine, why do you ask?"

"How many jobs have you had?"

"I don't..."

"How many jobs?"

"Four," the other man answered, feeling suddenly like a patient, scrutinised, prodded, poked. He didn't like the clammy feeling racing up his neck.

"And you are married, correct?"

He nodded.

"Parents alive?"

Again a nod, suspicion mounting behind.

"Bought a house?"

"Several," anger crept into his voice, "I really don't understand quite what you're driving at. Why are you asking me these questions?"

The doctor leant back, hands coming to rest on the arms of the leather chair. He thought for a moment and then, seemingly satisfied, spoke.

"I estimate that you have experienced at least six major life events over the space of your life," he said, "and..."

"Now just wait a minute, who are you to..."

"Please, let me finish."

The authority in that *'please'* made Ken's father fall silent.

"It is my estimation that you have undergone one significant experience every eight years on average. Your son, however has not even lived through one cycle of eight years. He is six years old."

"So tell me something I don't know," Ken's father whispered under his breath.

The doctor looked at him a little longer than comfort would allow. Eventually he continued.

"Kenneth can hardly be described as having lived a normal infanthood. From my sessions with him, I would assert that he has already undergone four significant events. The rigours of daily filming, the stop-start nature of the schedule, the absence of other children to whom he could relate, they have all taken a toll on his development. I am not sure you understand but Kenneth has missed an essential aspect of nurturing."

"I don't... I don't understand."

The doctor frowned.

"For Christ's sake man, do I have to spell it out for you? The mother and father have not been present during the early years of his psychological development. You have left him to develop in the hands of *television people*."

He spat this last out with some venom.

"We didn't..."

The doctor refused to let the excuse emerge.

"I'm afraid you did. If Kenneth is depressed it is because he has undergone change four times as fast as you yourself and in absence of any significant parental support. He tells me they used to give him medicine to calm him down between filming. Did you know that? I didn't think so. Do you know what that medicine was? No? Shall I explain in simple terms?"

The doctor stood and paced to regain his equilibrium. He'd been close to shouting. Long days spent with Kenneth in tears, complaining of headaches, of isolation, of remorse, of guilt, of mourning, of tiredness, of any number of symptoms classically indicative of severe adult stress weighted heavily upon him. What sort of parent could let this happen?

During the last session, Kenneth had grabbed him and hugged him hard, sobbing into his shoulder with huge, wracking, coughing splutters, like a toddler so enwrapped in his tantrum that he forgets to breathe.

And here was Kenneth's father, trying to justify how he could have left his son practically alone for six years and still expect to be called a father.

Just the one parent here.

It spoke volumes.

He turned back from the window, zeroed his gaze on the seated man.

"Where is your wife?"

"Huh?"

"Your wife. Where is she?"

"She's... She was... Unable to make it."

The doctor nodded.

"A long-standing appointment for the results of your son's psychological assessment, the end of four months of testing, of significant analysis and consultation and she was unable to make it. *Unable... To... Make... It.*"

"It's pathetic."

"Now hang on a minute..."

"No. This appointment is over. If you can trouble your wife to join you, we can reschedule to a more convenient time. Until then, I would advise you to spend time with your son to try and help him through the day."

"Help him through the day?" the bluster left his voice, "what do you mean *help him through the day?*"

The doctor walked back around his desk, sat down in his leather chair and leant forward again. After a long breath, he spoke.

"Valium," he said, "they gave him Valium in between scenes. He talks about sleeping. About how nice it would be to sleep for a long time. Your son is six and he speaks of sleeping to avoid people. The way he describes it... It's not... Let me read you this..."

The doctor pulled a sheaf of papers from the case-file on his desk. He riffled through until he came to the right page. When he spoke next, Ken's words emerged:

... sometimes when they're not looking sometimes I... I close my eyes and pretend I'm not there... They don't speak to me... they speak to me in the morning, though... if I sleep then they will speak to me... they will... If I sleep then... they can ignore me all they want... I won't care if they don't speak to me if I sleep...

"That is your son speaking. Verbatim."

He looked at the other man. At the grey colouring that had drawn his cheeks, momentarily making his face that of a ghost.

"Not only did they give your son a prescribed tranquiliser but in the process your son has, at the age of six, come to speak of suicide. A situation that you have allowed to happen."

"Oh, come on…"

The doctor referred to his notes once more.

... they can ignore me all they want... I won't care if they don't speak to me if I sleep...

"What is it that you do not understand? What are you not hearing? Your son is speaking clearly. You and your wife, wherever *she* is, just aren't listening."

"But I…"

"Good day, sir," the doctor said, slamming the case file and leaning back in his chair, "speak to my Secretary to confirm an appointment when you can both be present."

"But I…"

"Good day, sir."

Chapter 21:
Guest

They had all gone home, all the worker bees and copy-cat wannabes.

These offices weren't anything close to those of lower Manhattan hot-spots; this was Wall Street painted by numbers. So many corporations, so little space. As the island grew more congested, too expensive, they'd relocated over the Hudson. Endlessly structured all-staff meetings, talking up the free space of New Jersey, of how they could expand, of how the quality of life would be so much better. In search of the almighty WIIFM. All those empty promises, making it seem the solution for each and every colleague, partner, co-worker, team-mate; using any label but employee. So magnificent the spin that they might even have discovered the promised land.

Then they'd arrived.

And paradise had been no such thing.

I'd read all this in the newspapers when coming out here on previous car hunts, heard it in bars, overheard it in one-sided cell-phone rants. Eavesdropping helped me pass the time.

That evening, the streets were empty save for a passing car or two.

The gas station sat alongside an empty lot bounded by a scraggy chain-link fence, topped with barbed wire; a car park for the financial services giant across the road. Made me wonder what it was that they were trying to keep out of the lot. Or in. The concrete was cracked and patched almost beyond repair; the best that the financial giant was willing to do for its people.

Come to Jersey, where the quality of working life is so much better than the city... Come to Jersey...

The corporate bullshit merchants hid in Manhattan Headquarters, using advertisers on Madison, consultants on Park. High-charging accountants gave them proof of the value equation whenever they asked. Those executives, they knew that Jersey was the right thing for the business – just not the right thing for them. So they'd stayed in the city while the riff-raff were forced out to this godforsaken concrete labyrinth.

Which was how this gas station had ended up here, surrounded by faceless skyscrapers that emptied like an old man's diarrhoea at the end of every day, spilling into cars and SUVs and trucks and trains and buses and just about any mode of transport that could get them away from here and back across the river, or out into the country as quickly as possible.

This gas station made a fortune undoubtedly, just like the human traffickers who helped Eastern European women escape to the west. Desperate people will always pay money.

Besides, gas was a lot cheaper over here than in the city.

Another great reason to come to Jersey!

I settled into the doorway of a deserted tower, knowing that security wouldn't be checking outside, that the cameras were being ignored, that the underpaid guards would be busy playing cards or watching porn on the internet.

By eight p.m. I'd watched twenty or so cars come and go through the gas station.

It felt like my lucky night. Six of them left the keys in the car while they went into the station to buy something.

I had almost gone for the sixth but it had been a Lexus, and likely fitted with tracking. Almost definitely. Too easy for the police to spot once the alert went out.

The regularity of visiting customers began to decrease as the whole of this suburban city, come suburb, come city, come suburb emptied in its daily desertion ritual.

Almost all the rats had left the sinking ship.

The guy in the gas station would be shifting to *'through the window only'* service within the next half an hour.

I crossed the road, past the chain link lot, where I struck my bad rapper pose: a casual lean against the side of the gas station.

I could feel my heart beating as I lit up a cigarette; smoke clouding my face, filling my hoodie. I saw all of this like I was watching a movie, outside of myself and yet feeling the rush begin.

The Honda C-RV was so inconspicuous that I didn't really notice it until it turned into the station, pulled up at the pumps, stopped.

The woman who got out had curly red hair, down to the back of her neck. Dressed in a cheap suit, aping perfumed, coiffured doyens of the Upper East. Cheap meat dressed up to look like steak.

For a moment, my first ever mugging flew through my mind, the woman on the lower east, her pearls and evening dress, the way it had felt, and I knew that this would be my mark. Knew it in some instinctive way that got my blood pumping harder.

I smoked more rapidly, so that I could glance through the clouds in front of my face without catching her attention.

She was uncomfortable in her skirt. Kept hitching at it. Looked like she'd been wearing it all day and was just about sick of it. Something had been annoying her all day. Something. The skirt too tight for her. Used to fit her. Used to make her legs look good. Used to make her feel sexy. But now, in the heat, in the humidity, it just made her feel like a fat cow; past it, out to pasture. She was tired of pretending. Tired of playing the corporate game, tired of having to compete. Just tired. Period.

I got all of that from the way she picked and hitched at her skirt.

She didn't even look at me. Didn't even cast a glance in my direction.

Hooked the nozzle back into its cradle, grabbed the receipt from the pump and then opened her door, climbing into the car; I cursed my intuition for selling me blind. But the door didn't close, her foot emerging as she stepped out again, walking across the station's baked concrete, out of my sight and into the gas station.

My moment.

I was across the forecourt at a loping sprint, maintaining my rap persona, rolling my shoulders, exaggerating my black boy emphasis, making sure the cameras caught stereotype for posterity.

Over to the C-RV, its smoked windows, metallic paint and alloy wheel rims. Opened the door, jumped up into the driver's seat, turned the engine; this routine, so practised that I didn't even have to look. Keeping my eyes fixed on the station, watching her through the windows, stooping into the refrigerator cabinet, trying to find a Diet Coke or a Snapple or a Dr Pepper or whatever else it was she hoped would take the heat of a summer's evening away. So well rehearsed was I that I even noticed the guy behind the desk checking her ass as she bent into the cabinet.

He shook his head; dismissing her.

The engine spun and I pulled the transmission to drive, hitting the gas pedal at the same time, wheels spinning as I pulled out onto the road, turning hard right, heading around the block behind the gas station, immediately putting concrete and glass between myself and my victim.

I knew all this because I was an expert. I'd done this before. I'd learnt how to do this well.

I was almost a professional.

The adrenalin began to rush in and I howled like a wolf, a smile as bright as a death grin slathered across my face. I turned on the radio and punched the roof of the car in time to the music. It was some pop starlet but at that point I couldn't have cared less; the rush.

I maxed the volume, and the whole car shook with sub-bass. It was a good stereo. A good catch.

I wondered if I should head out into the country instead of just back over the river. That only lasted a minute though. Because I knew that the risk was just what it was: a risk. I had a full tank of gas, I had clear roads all the way across the George Washington Bridge, I had the night.

Across the next intersection, I brought the car down to the speed limit so as not to draw attention to myself. That too didn't last long; needle creeping up as adrenalin and the pumping music coerced my right foot. I slowed again; turned the volume down.

Buildings smeared past the windows of the car blurring the speed of light. I saw Subway become McDonalds become Chase Bank become Gap become an intersection, become a cop car...

I prayed. Prayed hard.

But he was looking the other way, must have been, because he wasn't even pulling out to follow me. I looked down and the dash showed me that I was only doing forty miles an hour, and that was why he wasn't following me. The buzz made my head do loops, made me feel like...

"Yes!" I shouted and punched the roof of the car again.

I'd cleared five miles already.

And the cop hadn't followed me.

Which meant the alert wasn't out yet. Which meant, as I eased onto the Garden State Parkway north that they wouldn't catch me. Not that night.

"Yes!" I shouted, pounding the roof over and over.

"Yes, yes, yes, yes, yes!"

I pulled out to overtake a truck that was riding the speed limit to the letter of the law.

"Yes!" A little voice from the back of the car.

"Whoa!" it came again, "big truck!"

The car almost went sideways as I turned to look.

But the child was right behind me.

Below my line of vision in the rear-view.

I got past the truck, pulled into the inside lane.

Breathing deeply despite the hammering of my heart.

"Bye-bye, truck," the child shouted gleefully, compounding my panic, inflating my shock.

"Bye-bye!"

My knuckles were tight on the wheel. Heart hammering. Gasping for air, searing down my throat.

A child! A fucking child!

Pull over, I thought, *I've got to pull over*.

But my foot stayed on the gas pedal. My eyes did anything but look back in the mirror.

How far back was that cop car? A mile? Two miles? Five?

The GW Bridge was only five miles ahead and I had a clear road; merciful given the usual state of Jersey traffic.

My eyelids fluttered and I felt like I was about to...

Chapter 22:
Family Rules – Part VI

In between scenes, I got to watch the filming on the monitors.

On the screen I watched the only people I knew as more than meaningless shapes; who didn't just come and go through my life taking something, asking for something or giving me something to keep me quiet.

These people on the monitors, I recognised their smiles, the way they held their heads when they were listening to each other, the way they all seemed to avoid honesty.

They laughed too loud.

They smiled too hard.

They glared behind each other's backs.

They whispered behind closed lips.

I saw all of this and it was my family. Every day on the monitors, I watched my mother and my father arguing with my grandpa and his paramour. Most days, I didn't know when I'd last seen my real mother and father.

I didn't even remember to let that hurt me.

*   *   *

"Are you crying?" Jamie asked, bending over the pushchair.

There was the noise of a baby crying. It wasn't me. I was watching the monitors. The baby in the pushchair was a dummy.

"Oh my lord," Martin said, winking at his onscreen son, "not only is she blind, she's deaf now too!"

Pause. Canned laughter.

"Obviously can't hear a thing!" Another wink.

Jamie bent over the pushchair, engrossed with a dummy that the camera couldn't see.

"I could just about say anything..." This time, Sanderson aimed the wink at the camera. It could not have been more telegraphed.

She was lifting the dummy, wrapped in woollen knitting.

"Go on love, do an old man a favour, eh? Get 'em out!"

Jamie dropped the dummy back into the pushchair. Stood upright. Hands on hips.

"You dirty old bugger," she said, "who d'ya think you're talking to, eh?"

"Oh I'm sorry," he said, all innocence and shrugs, "I didn't think you could hear me, so I just thought I'd.."

"Just thought you'd say what was on your mind, eh Dad?" His son chimed in.

Sanderson turned, paused, let the canned laughter respond to the look on his face.

"Whose side are you on?"

"Yeah," chimed Jamie, "whose side *are* you on?"

Cut to a wide shot, Jamie to the left, Sanderson to the right and the poor unfortunate boyfriend-son caught right in the middle.

It was a tug of war waiting to happen, the canned audience eager to see the denouement.

"*CUT!*" Joel's voice yelled from my left.

They turned as one to look at the director.

"Can't we do something about this fucking baby?"

And for a moment, I didn't know whether he was talking about me or the dummy or even whether I actually was the dummy.

"Huh?" Jamie's voice was loud in the silence.

Joel was up and pacing, heading towards the set.

"Well look at it!"

They did. It was lolling out of one side of the pushchair, arm bent at an alarming angle, eyes staring lifelessly at the ceiling ; or where the ceiling would have been if this were a real house rather than a television studio with about a million lights above the set, swinging from scaffold poles bolted to the roof.

"Oh."

"Yes, fucking well *Oh!*" Joel was furious. "Now we've got to redo the whole thing. Can't you be more careful how you drop it, Jamie?"

"I didn't mean to…"

"No, I bet you didn't," the director seething, his ire palpable even on the monitors, "can't we use the real one?"

"You're joking, right?"

"No."

"We can't drop a live baby…"

"Why not?"

"Because… Well… He's alive…"

"And that's why he won't end up looking like this pathetic little piece of worthless plastic…"

And with that, Joel kicked the dummy out of the pushchair. It flew end over end and smashed through a window on the other side of the couch.

"Oh fuck," Jamie hissed between her teeth.

"You said it," Sanderson concurred.

Joel went supernova.

Later that day, I was dropped into the pushchair when Martin suggested that Jamie go topless in order to test her hearing. I banged my head on the frame of the pushchair. It hurt a little. But I didn't care.

I'm a dummy. Nothing happens to me for real.

Nothing.

It's all just television.

Chapter 23:
Imagine All The People

I pulled off the Hudson at ninety-sixth and onto Riverside Drive, still full of panic and adrenalin from the George Washington Bridge, where there had been an unexpected, unpredicted breakdown on the far side of the tolls. It had kept me stuck in traffic for what was only five minutes but felt like hours; all the while lost in the memory of when I chose to run rather than remain with the car.

I'd been certain that the police were looking for me, that the automated close-circuit television cameras of the toll plaza would be keeping close watch for a CR-V stolen earlier that evening, the abducted child within. I broke into a sweat about twenty yards ahead of the tolls. Trying to work out what to do, whether to just get out and walk, whether to sit tight, knowing that the car had E-Zpass, that I could have gunned the engine and headed up that empty lane, but at the same time knowing that would have been absolutely the most stupid thing in the world to do given that I'd stolen the car and found out there was a kid in the back and why-oh-why would I just give them a tracking mechanism like E-ZPass to follow me by? All of which was immaterial anyway because by the time I'd gotten close enough to pay in cash, the E-ZPass had already waved me through, the attendant not even leaning out to talk to me; I was being tracked anyway.

I'd crawled past the breakdown, cursing to the high heavens, thankful that the kid was silent in the back.

I pulled the car over to the side of Riverside Park and sat, drenched in sweat, feeling my heart race and wondering what the hell I was going to do. I looked out over the basketball courts that fill with players every weekend from April to October, their cries and yells washing over people walking the Hudson, spending time in the sun, pretending that the city isn't behind them, that river is Riviera, that the air is actually fresh; parked to one side, in the shade of the trees, inconspicuous.

Thinking, *I could leave the car here.*

It would be found.

The child would be found.

I felt an itch begin at my temples. It was a safe enough part of Manhattan.

The child will be found.

I got out of the car, closing but not locking the door and began to walk. When I was far enough away, I planned to call the police and alert them to the car.

I walked.

Eighty-seventh.

And walked.

Eighty-second.

In my head the child was crying.

A shadow was falling over the side of the car. A junkie. Thinking it looked like it might be unlocked. Trying the handle. Opening the driver's door. Hearing the screaming. Knowing that there was probably money in the glove box. But there was a kid crying in the back. This kid wouldn't stop crying and it was just too much noise and the crack-head was aching for a fix and *wouldn't somebody just get that kid to stop crying.* He was reaching back, lifting his hand to strike and...

I tried to walk on but the compulsion to turn was too strong; the vision too clear.

I ran, breath burning my throat. Hoping that...

Stop. I should call the cops. I should...

But my feet were rebellious tonight and propelled me north, returning to risk, back into jeopardy.

And the CR-V was still in shadow. No-one near it.

The kid was crying. Screaming and I could hear it from twenty yards away, where I stood fighting breath back into my lungs.

The kid was screaming. Inconsolable.

I looked about myself, desperate to confirm that no-one else was witnessing this; the child's screams stood anything but mute witness to the abandoned nature of the street. Anyone hearing those cries would have been powerless but to respond.

I was powerless but to respond.

Walking up the street. Hoping that if I was being watched, the witness hadn't seen me walking away from the car about ten minutes earlier.

The child was screaming; garbled words and gasping sobs, grizzling, gulping for air.

I got to the car.

Looked through the window at the child's face, partially obscured by the tinted rear windows. Tears had streaked down its cheeks, mucky trails, parallel snot streamers glistening in what little streetlight got through the smoked glass. The child hugged some cuddly toy close to its chin, wracking out sobs that seemed to threaten its ability to breathe.

I should walk.

But my hand was on the door handle, pulling, finding it locked.

Me, the junkie of my vision.

The child seemed oblivious to the fact I was trying to open the door.

Screaming.

In my head, I was rehearsing what I would say when the inevitable passer-by walked up: *I don't know, I was passing and the car was parked and I heard this kid crying and I…*

I opened the driver's door, looked for the central locking, found the button and flicked it upwards, hearing the reassuring *thunk* of the locks releasing despite the sound of the child's screams.

I wished it would be quiet.

Wished I could have made it quiet.

But the child went on screaming.

And I was out, taking one final look up and down Riverside before opening the rear door, leaning in, looking at its face, the tears and snot and fear in its eyes and I was fumbling with the buckle on the car seat, trying to make sense of it when I realised it's like a back-pack with the two pieces of plastic and I tried it and *snap,* the thing was open and the kid was still screaming its head off and I tried to hook the straps over its shoulders and the kid just launched out of the chair in my direction, pushing with both of its legs, standing and twisting as it came flying at me, reaching out, ensnaring my neck and grabbing hold. I stood straight, bashing the back of my head on the doorframe, setting off a flare of pain and the child was slipping out of my arms because I hadn't gotten hold of it, my arms and hands flapped as they tried to grab hold but the kid was strong, clinging to my neck to stop itself falling and…

Anyone could have been watching this.

Move, a voice spoke in my head, *get out of here!*

The same voice that had spoken to me when I woke up in Washington Square with a dead body on the next bench.

And I began to run, the kid sobbing into my neck, clinging tight as I moved. Its head was hot. Bloody hot. I ran. The kid began to quieten down as I moved and as it relaxed, as whatever energy I had stored up in my underused muscles petered out, as my breath accelerated, growing laboured and gasping, I realised just how heavy it was. Still, I ran.

Some of the people I passed caught my eye but not so much more than they would were I sitting across from them on a subway train. New Yorkers. Able to consciously ignore anything out of the ordinary. One or two of them even gave me a look of consolation: *tough bringing up a child in the city, isn't it?*

I slowed to a walk a block from Central Park. More from exhaustion than any rational response to the situation; I was long past caring whether I drew attention to myself or not. Across Central Park West and I was entering the park through Strawberry Fields. I had no choice but to sit down on the first bench I passed; my arms burned with the weight of the kid. Burned.

The kid kept clinging to my neck even when I'd sat down.

Over its head and shoulder, I stared at the black and white circular mosaic: *Imagine*.

The kid's hair was stuck to my face where I was sweating, strands of it in my mouth.

Some hippy freak was playing a Beach Boys song about five benches around the circle: *Sloop John-B*. There were flowers on the memorial, dry from being there all day, withered now, petal flakes dropped all around where the breeze had denuded dying blooms. I looked up to my right and there was the Dakota, where Lennon was shot and I was sitting holding a fucking child I had accidentally abducted from fucking New Jersey.

A kid who had grown silent in my arms.

As the hippie played *Sloop John-B*, I began to cry a little.

What was I going to do?

What the fuck was I going to do?

*   *   *

In the end, I just walked. Carrying the kid across the park. Stopping every so often to sit on a bench. After a while, I realised that the kid was actually asleep. I looked at my watch. It was past eleven. No wonder.

All I could think about was getting to the apartment, where I could at least hide behind a closed door. And think.

I needed to think.

*　　*　　*

I got through the door, my arms feeling like molten steel. It felt like I wouldn't be able to unlock my fingers from where they were entwined beneath the kid's butt.

Stumbled into my room, legs turning to jelly, arms burning and, like a memory that keeps playing in my head – of Jamie on the monitors, of a dummy I thought was me – I dropped the kid on the bed.

It bounced a couple of times but ended up on its side, still asleep.

Cramps set into my arms and I rubbed at the muscles, trying to ease the knots tightening there; pain and potential for relief even obliterating the panic that assailed my every thought.

My legs started to shake and I felt like I was about to puke. I twisted to sit on the corner of the bed near the pillow; reaching out to gain comfort from the notches on my headboard post, the count of cars I have stolen.

Knowing that night had seen my final notch.

A whimper from behind as the child stirred, rolling over. I turned to look and before I could react, watched it tumble off the bed and onto the floor.

Its eyes opened.

It looked about itself.

My stomach hit my shoes as I anticipated the scream, the tears, the yells, the guilt. The panic had never strayed too far. I *was* about to puke. I felt it rising in my gorge.

And then the child looked at me. Looked directly at me.

"Truck," it said and closed its eyes again, resting its head on its arm on my bedroom floor.

I sat and watched it sleep, too tired to move a muscle and scared that if I did I'd just end up on my knees on the floor, losing my lunch and whatever else the panic could find within me.

I couldn't tell whether the kid was a boy or a girl. It began to snore slightly as it drifted deeper asleep and as I watched and listened and tried to work out what I was going to do, my own eyelids began to droop and I was fading away and I didn't know whether it was a boy or a girl and it was hard to tell because I hadn't put the light on so I was only getting half light and was it a boy or a girl or...

I jolted upright.

I'd know soon enough what sex it was. I'd know its name. Its mother's name. Its father. I'd know where they lived and what they did for work and I'd know their scared, tearful faces and I'd hear them beseeching whoever took their baby just to return it safe if they were watching, please just bring our baby back to us safe...

I should have turned on the television to see this. I should have. But I was tired. I was so, so tired.

I picked the kid up off the floor in a daze, put it in the middle of my bed then, rolling alongside it, I fell asleep; blissful oblivion that I would cling to for however long I could to avoid waking.

*   *   *

During the early hours of the morning, I surfaced from an already forgotten dream. Heard someone breathing, slight snoring.

Drifted back to sleep, comfortable in another's presence.

* * *

The curtains let in a little light; colours and warmth, familiar smells, sanctuary.

Pleasant thoughts drift through my mind, making me smile, making me feel all warm at my core, like hot soup on a cold, cold day, like bread rising in the oven, the smell of it wafting through the house, like coffee and roses.

Warmth.

I bask in the glow, knowing that I don't have to get out of bed yet, that I don't have to disturb this moment; this peace.

The dream I had last night, the dark dream, the one that woke me briefly, sweating from where I'd been fighting against some other, some thing, some dark presence that chased me down alleyways and darkened streets, carrying something that shone, something that shimmered, something that could slice at a moment's notice, that dream is gone; merciful release, tatters of terror in my waking moments.

Ah, but this warmth. It supplants the fear, drives it out, water under oil, lifting it, forcing it above and away. My nightmare became the sky, so broad and high that I have no fear of it falling.

I hear the breathing, in and out, in and out, breathing. Take it in my head to go and check, get out of bed, grab something familiar, reminding me of warmth as I choose to stray beyond the confines of my sublime room; tethered to the taste of toffee ice cream.

I walk into the hall, turn left, towards their bedroom. Walk, carrying my special something.

The door is pulled to but I hear breathing, in and out, fast and slow, in and out. I place a hand on the door and push.

They are a single mound in the middle of the bed, beneath sheets and comforter, a single being, moving in time to the rhythm of their cacophonic breathing.

My warmth is still with me and I want to share it, I so badly want to share it with them. I cross to the bed, stretch up, grab hold of the sheets and pull myself up, plopping down on my father's side of the bed. They keep moving, keep writhing, keep rising and falling and falling and rising and I sit and watch the covers inflate and deflate – cotton lungs – forwards and back and they are lost in their rhythm and their breathing and he's groaning and she's reciprocating and they are flying in each other for a moment, together in a way that their frost prevents the rest of the time and I am listening to their breathing, gradually feeling the warmth of my sanctuary leaving me the longer I stay away from my room, more distant from that fullness, the goodness that filled me when I woke to find my nightmare above the ceiling, far, far away, far…

"Ken!" *my father screams, looking out from under the cover,* "what the fuck are you doing here? What the fuck? GET OUT!"

It scares me so rigid that I can't move, for the moment my nightmare has tumbled through the sky, through the clouds, through the roof and is in front of me; snarling, teeth bared in a grimace.

"Huh?" I hear her ask, lost in a daze, reporting in from another planet.

"GET OUT!" *he reiterates and now my freeze has gone. I jump from the bed and run back down the hall, diving back to my room, hoping to find the warmth I'd left behind. I run around my bed, to the small gap on the other side, near the window, the gap where I play hide and seek with imaginary friends, lying for what seems hours only to find that there's no-one to find me but me. I lie down now, not understanding what I've seen, why he shouted at me, why he screamed at me.*

I begin to cry.

Softly, for fear he'll hear me, know where I'm hiding.

I don't even stop when I realise that my favourite teddy is back in there with him, where I left it on the bed.

For a moment, a thought goes through me that I am powerless to prevent: good, maybe ted will get it instead of me. Maybe.

I don't know how long I stay there, how long I wait, dreading the sound I eventually hear. His footsteps in the hallway. By the time they tread my bedroom carpet, I am actually whimpering, unable to stop myself. I hear him come around the bed. Able to see me. No doubt about it. Looking down on me, lying here, face down on the carpet, whimpering and blubbering and terrified of the look on his face, the grimace, the snarling teeth and he is looking down on me, looking down like a statue, like a nightmare that has superseded the clouds, usurped the sky, obliterated the horizon. He is standing and I am crying and...

His hand touches my arm, gets hold of my tiny six year old bicep, pulls me to my feet, turns me to face him as easily as if he'd been picking up a bag of shopping.

I daren't look at him, stare at my bed, the colours and patterns and cartoon animals, stuffed toys ranged as territorial markers.

"Ken," he says forcefully and I recoil at the sound of his voice, maintain my stare, keep it locked on the toys.

"Kenny," more gentle this time, easing back, maybe getting a sense of how terrified I am, how he has scared me beyond a nightmare of knives and slashing, "Kenny?"

His hand beneath my chin, turning my face to his and I can smell something coming off him, something like fish or sweat; an odour he's always had on him, varying only in its level of intensity. I try and fight against making contact with those hate-filled eyes, try and avoid his stare, refuse to take in the emotion that's written all over his face.

But I cannot resist and eventually I have to look at him.

And see some level of fear mirrored there.

In his other hand, he holds my teddy by one of its worn, six year-old cloth paws. He senses me looking, I think, seems to remember the toy in his hand, looks at me, back at teddy, back at me, shoves the bundle of rags and make-believe eyes at me as a peace offering.

"Here," he says.

I am shaking, still terrified that this is the calm between two storms. I remember the white of his teeth, flecks of spit flying as he screamed my name.

"Kenny," he speaks and my shaking amplifies, "your mother and I... We were..."

My teeth hurt from where I'm grinding them together.

"We were... er... dancing..."

He stares nonplussed at my nonplussed expression. I don't know what he's talking about. I don't understand.

"We were... When two puh...people..." he stammers, losing his thread.

I stare at him, gaining the smallest sense that he may not hold all the cards after all. I might survive this. I might.

"You aren't normally up this early," pursuing a different track, heading towards the same dead end, "we don't normally see you until seven-thirty or so and we... Er... We..."

The dead end arrives.

I take the opportunity to draw my arm across my eyes, wiping the tears and the snot from my face, hearing snuffling and sniffling, knowing that the nightmare isn't that far away after all.

"You shouted at me," I say, voice choking around a huge lump in my throat.

"Sorry," he says quietly.

"I was scared," I say, hugging my teddy bear and laying it plain in front of him.

"You scared me."

* * *

I didn't dream. I didn't run scared in a nightmare. I didn't come gradually back to the world, with the sunlight on my eyelids and that cosy feeling of warmth under blankets.

It didn't take me but a moment to remember what happened last night.

I was sharing my bed with a little kid that I had abducted.

It was still sleeping.

Thank God, it was still sleeping, facing away from me, head buried in the crook of its arm.

I stood from the bed and my heart was already racing with panic. Through the apartment to the living room, switched on the television, hunted down CNN and just sat there on the couch, watching, waiting.

Nothing.

Pretty soon, the couch grew uncomfortable. I crossed to one of the chairs by the dining table. Sat there until the couch became attractive again. Went back over there and the presenter still wasn't talking about a child having been abducted.

I guess when there are bombings and murders and questionable invasions of far flung places where hate-filled eyes claim holy war and behead in the name of everything that's good, what's another child gone missing?

In the bedroom, the kid slept on.

Chapter 24:
Learn

My first day of education in the new continent covered me in solitude.

Our apartment, familiar confines, endless walls.

My parents would be gone before I woke, father out to work and mother out to breakfast with her Upper East cronies; Seventy-sixth crones. Me, waking up to no note on the fridge and an *au pair*, Camille, who couldn't care less that I was stood in the middle of the kitchen dressed in a t-shirt and underpants, wondering where the hell my breakfast was.

Demanding my breakfast.

We'd been in New York for a little over three months.

I decided to throw a tantrum.

Whether by design or otherwise, my parents had moved us in the late Spring, with Summer yawning ahead. No school.

Every day, they'd sit Camille down when they got home, monitoring reality: *how's he been, what's he said, how's he feeling, what's he broken?* All reported by live-in help, received after a long day in the office chair, modern saddle, just as leathery though twice as hard.

Throughout June to August, thanks to careful childcare and absent parents, I received a strict ration of two afternoons a week in Central Park.

All the time, Camille would be talking with the other hired help, calling out to me only when it looked like I would hurt myself, running some risk of bringing her liability into question.

My sixth summer, burnt in boredom, self-absorption and the sense that I had stolen the UK from my parents, that I'd been the problem, that I was wrong.

I was wrong.

So when it came time to arrange for me to go to school, they really hadn't thought twice about it. Of course, they'd made a play of discussing schools with me, sharing the options, speaking for me, to me, making my mind up, making my decision, making me believe that I was wrong for making them have to go through this.

"Public schools are…"

"You'd like to go to…"

"Camille says… knows what she's talking about…"

"… lot's of really nice kids… your friends, they'll all be interested to meet…"

"…you'd love to have a private tutor, wouldn't you?"

And like that, it had been decided. I wasn't to go to school. I wasn't to meet other kids. I wasn't to have a communal education.

"Today is the first day of the rest of your life."

They told me that when I was six years old.

He told me.

Already reduced to banalities and ad-line hooks.

The next day, my new tutor arrived at the door of our apartment, welcomed by Camille, ushered in without ceremony to a table she didn't own and a kid who wasn't hers, following orders left by parents who couldn't be bothered to be around for this excruciating, terrifying introduction.

When my tutor walked in.

When I was standing in the kitchen.

When Camille looked at me.

I'd wet my underpants.

*   *   *

I lied when I said that I'd made the blasé choice to start using hard drugs.

It was a lie.

All right.

I lied.

*   *   *

Watching CNN, seeing headline stories cycle past – a dead body here, a murder there, political faux pas and economic catastrophe in the Mid-West – I found myself thinking of Ivvy, of a couple of nights earlier, our stupid argument over that book, *The Earth From The Air*, and how it had made me feel and I was thinking that if there was one person I wanted to call right now, it was Ivvy, my confidante, my partner-in-crime, my junkie soulmate. All I could thinkwas that there was no way she would be willing to listen, to understand that I didn't mean it.

No way would she listen.

No way would she understand.

I didn't mean it.

I did not mean it.

*   *   *

The kid started screaming in the bedroom and my eyes snapped back to focus from where the television screen had become a blur; lost in thoughts of calling Ivvy.

The kid was screaming like there was no tomorrow.

And I heard a key in the door.

Oliveria.

And the kid was screaming.

I dashed.

The front door opening. Her shadow falling over the wall where the hallway light envelopes her. The door pushing wide.

Plastic bags rustled together as she gathered them from the floor.

I darted into my room, shutting the door behind me.

"Kenneth?" I heard her say to the empty hallway.

She hadn't expected me to be there, more used to my being at Ivvy's, knowing that my parents and I were strangers who crossed paths in the apartment on a random basis.

The kid was taking a breath and, as I leaped towards the bed, I shouted.

"In here!"

I slammed my hand tight over the kid's mouth, feeling its breath hot against my palm.

Oliveria didn't reply; hadn't heard me.

The kid yelled, but I held tight over the screams.

For a moment, it crossed my mind that I could easily have lifted my hand over its nose.

Held tight.

Tight.

It screamed harder and I realised I was pushing its head back into the covers.

Terrified. Eyes huge. Absolutely huge; all whites with seemingly tiny blue discs amid the snowy wastes.

I loosened my hand a bit but it was still screaming.

"Ken?" Oliveria, outside my bedroom door.

I looked at the kid.

"Shhhhh," I mouthed at it, thinking as fast as the adrenalin would allow, panic fluttering in my chest and behind my eyes, "shhhhh…"

But the child didn't quieten. Not one bit.

"Ken?"

"In here," I said, too scared to yell, too hyped to whisper, "I'm in here."

"Como està," she asked through the door.

"Fine," I said, all false positivity, "just fine."

"Bien?"

"Yup!"

"Oh… OK…" She didn't sound convinced.

The child's eyes were terrified.

"Look at me," I said quietly, forcefully.

It looked towards the door.

"At me," I spit, "look… at… me…"

And it turned its head, looked at me.

And I looked back into baby blues and dread and fear and panic and alarm and…

"Quiet," I hissed through clenched teeth. "Just be quiet."

It got the message, gradually easing off to the point where I tentatively lifted my hand from over its mouth.

I was shaking. Remembering what it had felt like when I'd thought about lifting my hand over its nostrils. How close I'd been to doing so. Close.

"There," I said as calmly as I could, "that wasn't so hard, was it?"

The child lay on its back, whimpering quietly. I knelt there on the bed, listening to the noise of Oliveria getting ready to clean the apartment, knowing from previous experience that she wouldn't try to clean my room if I told her *not today*. Knowing all this and yet wondering once again just what I was going to do.

What the fuck was I going to do?

* * *

"Hello," he said, smiling at me, "I'm Robin. Robin Norris."

Stooped to offer me a hand.

Looked down.

Saw the wet stain spreading across the material of my underwear.

"Oh dear," he said, voice rapidly filling with distaste.

"I'm sorry..." I burbled, close to tears.

"Yes, well..." he made a brave job of continuing.

"I'm sorry," the tears broke free, "I'm sorry, I'm sorry, I'm sorry!"

"Kenneth!" Camille admonished me.

But I was lost in my reverie of disgust, terror, revulsion. Lost in the fear of this strange man, his voice so like that of my father, so clipped, so British, so full of blame for who I was, for what I was, for every bad thing I'd bought upon my parents in the sad, small time I'd had on Earth. I was lost.

I was sinking.

I started to scream.

* * *

I opened the door a crack, leaned out, listened for Oliveria; sounds from the kitchen.

"Oliveria?" I said, conscious that the child was still whimpering every now and then behind me.

"Ken?" she replied, still banging things together in the kitchen.

"Yup," I said, putting on my best *I'm sick* voice, "can you keep it down a bit, please? I'm not feeling so good."

Her head appeared around the doorframe, took a long look at me. Appraised me. Tested me. Eventually, she nodded without a word and turned back into the kitchen.

I retreated into my room.

Shut the door, leaned my back against it and slid down until I was sitting on the floor. Looked at the child, face down in the middle of my bed, hands to its eyes as if warding off a bad dream, crying softly into its palms.

Eventually, it looked up at me, checking me out, sizing me up. Fear was large in that face. Those eyes.

I didn't know what to do. This terrified child staring at me. Staring.

Staring.

"Hello," I said, quietly.

It said nothing.

"I'm..."

It stared.

"I'm Ken," I said, the only thing that came to my mind.

Television images flashed through my mind.

Family Rules! videos that my parents brought over, that I'd watched accompanied by therapist after therapist trying to unpick what was my real experience versus that of my make-believe family; the damage done by confusing the difference.

"What's your name?" I asked.

"Ken?" I heard Oliveria ask from the other side of the door.

Shit.

"You talk to someone?"

I don't need this, Oliveria, I don't need this.

"On... On the phone," I said, coughing a couple of times to try and maintain the pretence of illness.

"Oh," she said and I heard her retreating down the hall; feeling like a kid caught out by parents who cared enough to check.

The other kid in the room just stared at me.

Blond hair messy from where it had slept on it, clots of sleep gunk in the corner of its eyes, dried snot all over its lower face from the crying.

I smiled, trying my best to make my face open and honest.

"Come on," I coaxed, "what's your name? Tell me?"

It shook its head slightly, still scared.

How old was this kid?

It had spoken last night. In the car. A couple of words.

But...

I pointed at my chest.

"Ken."

Nodded my head, tapped my chest, nodded again.

"Kenny."

It drew breath, about to speak and then closed its mouth again. Said something so quiet that I only heard a breath. But it had been something like Dave or Dan, definitely a D, that much I had caught.

"Are you Dan?" I asked, trying for the confirmation.

It shook its head.

"Dave?"

Again the shake, a slight smile beginning to spread across its lips.

Was it playing a game with me? It couldn't be, surely?

"Are you sure your name isn't Dan?" I said, playfulness in my tone.

It shook its head again but this time, frowned.

"Damp," it said clearly.

I even got chance to wonder how a kid could get a name like that before thoughts collided, slamming into place.

The kid was in diapers and hadn't had a change since the previous night.

Damp.

I began to panic all over again.

Chapter 25:
Family Rules – Part VII

When I was a little over four years old, my father built me a tree-house. Not just a little platform in a tree, this was a sixteen-by-sixteen deck, raised above the ground on stilts, the tree forming one corner; built on a hill, the lowest side only four feet off the ground, with the other at least eight feet high.

He worked weekend after weekend in the heat and humidity, sweating and cursing and sweating and cursing but all the time, building, building, building. When he added the fire-pole for me to slide down, he couldn't have been more proud, shouting from the garden that I should come down and look, come down and play. All the time, behind his words the simplest of statements: *look at me, look at what a great father I am.*

I love you.

Smiling, laughing, waiting for my reaction.

At which point I turned to the camera, frowned and said, *"Is that post straight?"*

The audience melted.

His crestfallen expression was comedy condensed.

* * *

Season four, episode six.

Episode six.

The tree-house.

The first time the whole thing centred on me rather than Jamie.

The first time I stole the show.

*   *   *

The fire-pole was great – reaching out to it, stretching across a gap that felt like it was always going to be that bit too far, that my fingertips would barely touch cool metal before the chasm swallowed me; a moment's panic then the plunge. But suddenly, contact! Two hands on the pole, cautionary words from a hyperventilating adult minder, and I was leaping, wrapping my legs around the metal.

Slide!

At the bottom, I stepped off, turning around to shout, "Do it again!"

My minder said no, that they had to rearrange the shot and get ready for Jamie's entrance.

Escorted to the trailer across the lot that I shared with my co-stars; days spent gazing at half-empty bottles of gin and vodka, cigarette butts overflowing assembled ashtrays, a weird smell that felt a little like home.

I was four years old.

*   *   *

Season four, episode six.

Episode six.

The first time I got to speak on camera.

Sure, I'd gurgled and burbled and smiled my way through to now, learning just what they wanted me to do by responding to offered rewards.

Pavlov didn't have anything on Joel and the rest of the Gestapo he employed to keep the talent in line.

"Is that post straight?"

My first spoken line ever.

It had been written down for me, my own typed page where it was underlined and emphasised in bold.

If only I'd been able to read.

I was four years old.

*   *   *

I sat on the bottom step of the trailer, the single type-written page clutched in my hand. I'd been sitting there alone for what felt like ages, just sitting, looking at the letters, looking at the letters, trying to make them make sense. Under my breath, a mantra, I spelled the words.

I...

S...

T...

Looked around myself, spotted my minder, over at the other end of the trailer, speaking with some guy I didn't know who wore a black t-shirt; *T... H... E... C... U... R... E...* spelled out on it. I didn't know what that meant but I knew the letters. I could read them *all myself.*

I looked back at the paper in my hand.

I...

S...

T...

H...

I was shaking. Shaking. Trying to work out what it said. Trying to work out what they wanted me to say. Ever since that guy, the other one, had stopped by the trailer and knocked at the door, ever since my minder had welcomed him in and taken the bit of paper, smiling at him and just... Smiling at him... I'd been trying to work it out.

There were no ringing bells for me to respond to this time.

What did they want me to say?

I...

S...

"Kenny? Are you all right?"

I looked up into the sunlight and Jamie was standing there, a shadow towering above me. My eyes snapped back to the crumpled page.

"I..."

Don't know what to say.

Am sorry.

Am scared.

Am frightened.

Love you.

Don't want to be here.

Am sad.

"I..."

She squatted down by my side until she could look me in the eye, reaching out, her fingers beneath my chin, tilting my head up. I stared at the page. Stared at it.

"What's up, Kenny?"

"S..."

"Are you reading?"

"T..."

My eyes burned a hole through the paper.

"Kenny?"

"H…"

Now I began to cry. Blurting it out and shuddering with the force of it. Through watering eyes, I saw that my minder hadn't even noticed. A tear dripped onto the page; in amongst the crumples and smudged ink it set up capillary action, blurring as it spread.

Jamie sat next to me on the step, pulled me close, held me tight, resting her chin on the top of my head, her voice soothing, calming me down.

"There, there, there, there…"

And I sobbed into the material of her shirt, sobbed and sobbed and sobbed and all the time, breaking through the sadness and the panic and the fear and the tears and the utter and complete screaming mess that was going on in my head, I was spelling.

I… S… T… H… A… T…

* * *

When I turned to the camera to speak the words, I heard Jamie's voice in my head.

"It says *Is that post straight?* Kenny, nothing more than that. That's all you have to say."

I'd mumbled it into the material of her shirt, damp from my tears, warm from her body beneath; I could have dived into that softness, that beating heart, succour and comfort.

"You don't need to be worried."

I turned, remembering what Joel had told me.

"Don't you dare smile, all right?"

I turned, remembering all the instructions and direction but most of all Jamie's voice.

"You don't need to be worried."

I turned to the camera, stared right into it. For the first time, stared into its unblinking, cool, glimmering refraction; reflections of enhanced sunlight cast from studio lamps on metal stands. I stared into the bottomless, shining blackness of the lens. Stared.

Stared.

Raised one eyebrow, quizzical, heard Jamie's words in my head. Delivered them in my own voice.

"Is that post straight?"

And Joel yelled *CUT!* But I kept looking deep into the heart of oblivion; safety.

I'd spoken to the camera.

Into the camera.

Deep into the nothing.

Finally I looked away.

Joel was watching me. Chris was watching me. Jamie was watching me.

It was Joel who broke the silence, with uncharacteristic rapture.

"Jesus fucking H Christ!" he shouted, staring at me, waving his hand at some minion over his left shoulder. "Did we get it? Did we get it?"

A mumble. *Yup, we got it.*

I stared at them. Seeing only the black centre of the camera's lens, its depth, it's absolution.

"Did I get it right?" I mumbled.

They were all smiling. I must have got it right. All of them, except Jamie. Her face was smiling but her eyes; there was something else in them. She knew something had just happened. Knew it.

She looked away.

Chapter 26:
Pants on Fire

Years later, looking down at a child who, in turn, looked up at me, I was back in the camera's dark eye, in the escape I'd felt in being no-one. I remembered Jamie's eyes, the warmth of her comfort, the half-smile that didn't provide the veneer she'd planned.

And in her eyes, the guarded emotion that I'd never truly put my finger on until that moment. *Threat.*

I looked down at the child, hearing Oliveria off somewhere, clanking and crashing her way through the apartment, and thought hard on what I should do.

Comfort.

Threat.

Escape.

Swirling, swirling, swirling.

That moment I'd stared into the camera, losing myself in it's oblivion. Giving myself away. Becoming someone else.

Comfort.

Becoming someone else.

I could become someone else.

Jamie's eyes.

I could become someone else.

I could be your father.

Your tears in the car. The way you'd leapt from the seat into my arms. The warmth and heaviness when we sat and listened to the hippy in Strawberry Fields. When I held you like Jamie had held me.

I could be your father.

I could be your father.

I will be your father.

*   *   *

Oliveria clanked and clunked away elsewhere in the apartment, a vacuum cleaner roaring, the television on, turned up to accompany the melee.

And I was staring at a tousle-haired, half-awake child, looking up at me, terrified yet somehow nonchalant.

"Damp," it said to ram home the point.

I can act this out, my thoughts declared, *I can be someone else.*

I look down at the kid and knew that I could act the role of its father. Even if it was only to get it as far as the local precinct.

Running across the Upper West with that child in arms; sympathetic looks and apathy. Sitting in Strawberry Fields; nostalgia songs. No-one giving a second thought to father and child.

I could do that.

But first I had to prepare, get myself into role.

Get the kid some diapers.

*   *   *

"Do you want to take that off?"

A nod.

"Is it damp?"

Another. A look in its eyes.

Stupid fucking question, you idiot.

"Can you do it?"

A nod and the kid started to take its pants down. The diaper was huge, swollen, distended.

The kid – the girl – pulled the diaper down and stepped out of it. Looked up at me.

"Is that better?"

It seemed I had nothing but questions.

She nodded.

"Oh... OK..."

She stared at me.

"I'll get another one, don't worry," I bumbled, "I just need to... to..."

What?

This is New York, you idiot, I chided myself.

No-one shopped on the Upper East, no-one sullied their feet by stepping into a supermarket. Not when there was a telephone and a host of illegal immigrants willing to earn a quarter for delivery.

"I'll dial out for some."

*   *   *

I stepped out of my bedroom, immersing myself in the cacophony that was our cleaning lady in full flight. I was wearing the bracelet she'd bought me around my wrist, so ingrained that I generally didn't notice it's there. But I did now.

I placed the heel of my palm against my right eyebrow, stooped a bit and walked through to the living room, where she was polishing ornaments, clinking them down on the glass-topped table.

Acting again.

Becoming someone else.

"Oliveria?" I said through clenched teeth, "Oliveria?"

She looked up at me.

"Si?"

And the way she looked at me – like Jamie, like Camille, like anyone but my own mother – I felt caught out, transformed into an insect that dared to walk among mammals. She knew. She knew.

I chose understatement over Broadway.

"I've got a bad migraine... Any chance you could come back another time?"

She looked at me. No emotion, no capitulation.

I fought the urge to squirm.

Closed my eyes, drew breath on a hissed inhalation.

"You have migraine?"

She asked.

No, I thought.

"Yes," I said.

She stood, tossing her cloths into the cleaning bag she'd brought with her.

Without a word, she moved through the apartment, gathering her tools, making sure that the areas she'd already completed were squared away. Finally, satisfied, she regained her coat from where it was hanging in the hallway closet. She walked to the door. Opened it. All the time, so quiet, such a church mouse, just to save my imaginary headache.

Standing in the hallway, she looked at me where I leant against the door, ushering her out, shadowing her until she was off the property.

Her eyes spoke of distrust and calculation.

My heart sank. I hadn't played the role well enough. Anyone with a migraine would have been in bed by now, even if they'd felt strong enough to speak to someone.

I hoped she hadn't realised.

I hoped...

No. I would act like she hadn't realised.

"I'm sorry, Oliveria," I said, almost whispering. "Sorry that you came over for nothing. I wish I'd had chance to call you."

She shrugged, *de nada*.

De nada.

I'd heard that before.

"I need to sleep," I said and it wasn't so far from the truth.

And suddenly, Oliveria was smiling. Broad. Ear to ear.

I fought down the unbidden image of the wino on the park bench, neck opened in a grin to end all grins.

"Kenneth," she said, winking in conspiratorial camaraderie, "if you want to be alone with her, why you no say so?"

My brain did a back-flip. I'd been awake when she'd arrived. I *had* been. She couldn't have seen the kid. Couldn't have...

"Don't know what you're talking about," I said, growling with imagined pain, "I've got to..."

She reached out, placed a hand on my arm, looked me straight in the eye.

"You are young man," she said, smiling, "you should not be alone while your parents are away. You need someone with you."

She smiled.

"I am happy to leave the two of you alone."

She had no idea quite how happy that made me. And the fact that she was presuming I had a fuck-buddy in my room just made it better.

I put on my best mock-embarrassed face, dropping the migraine shtick.

"Goodbye, Oliveria," I said, "thanks for everything."

I shut the door in her face. Turned and ran to the living room, changing the channel to CNN, speed-dialling the store on the corner of our block.

"Diapers, diaper cream, baby milk... What? Baby milk... Huh? Yes, formula... Formula, yes. And some biscuits and baby food and... What? Well how would I know? What? Jars... Definitely jars... Oh I don't care, you choose!"

I recited the address. They told me twenty minutes. I hung up.

Walked to the bedroom.

"We'll have your diapers in twenty minutes," I said. Then I turned back towards the living room without waiting for a response.

After all, I was sure that I'd just seen her mother giving a press conference on CNN.

Chapter 27:
Misfire

Turned out it wasn't the kid's mother. Some woman down in Washington trying to secure her future reality television career by accusing a congressman of sharing pillow talk secrets. The second oldest profession: *making a name off the oldest*.

I breathed.

For what felt like the first time since I'd driven away from the gas station the night before I breathed.

A shuddering, shaking, tremulous breath deep into my lungs.

I picked up the phone.

An ad for Larry King cycled across the screen; a cadaverous relic of the eighties, replayed every weeknight, nine to ten p.m. for almost twenty years.

I dialled Ivvy's number.

* * *

She didn't answer for the longest time. Time enough for me to watch the end of the ads, to get my breathing under control.

When she spoke, it was clear I'd woken her.

"Yeah?" she grated in my ear.

I almost put the phone down but spoke before I could deliver on that impulse.

"Ivvy, I…"

"What the fuck do you want, asshole?" Now she was alert, fully awake, ready to bring me down.

"I need to…"

"Shut up and listen! What the fuck was that last night? One minute we're looking at that fucking book and then you're storming out and I don't know what the fuck you're doing or what I've don…"

"Ivvy."

"I mean what the fuck were you thinking about? Huh? Assh…"

"Shut up."

"What?" She was incandescent. But I couldn't let her have this moment. I needed it.

"Shut up. I need you to listen."

She must have heard it in my voice.

"OK?"

"OK?"

"OK."

"I need your help. Something really… Really… Can you get over here?"

"What, *now?*"

"Yeah, now."

"This had better be good," she said and put the phone down.

Leaving me to wait for the delivery of baby supplies.

Watching CNN for reports on the kid.

* * *

It was only when the buzzer sounded and I had to get up to release the door that I realized I hadn't moved for almost twenty minutes.

Hadn't moved.

Hadn't spoken.

Hadn't listened.

Hadn't thought of checking on the kid because my thoughts had been filled with the kid.

Filled with ideas and plans that verged on fantasy.

I'd decided that I didn't want Ivvy to know after all.

I buzzed the delivery guy into the building and went to check on the girl.

*   *   *

More questions.

"Is that OK?"

"It's not too tight?"

"Do you want to put your pants on?"

"What's your name?"

*   *   *

I called Ivvy on her cell-phone – she answered on the second tone.

"What?" she said, traffic roaring in the background.

"Don't bother," I replied, "it's all right now."

I lied.

"Huh?" I knew that, wherever she was, she'd just stopped dead in her tracks.

My brain scrambled for some reason, some excuse, some something to try to ease her down from the inevitable rage. My mouth didn't seem to realize this was happening and forged on regardless.

"I thought I needed you."

And this time it was my turn to stop breathing. The living room swam about me for a moment.

I ended the call without another word, dropping the handset on the couch.

My hand rubbed the twenty year old scar that sits beneath my eyebrow.

In my head, the chair flying through the air.

In my ears, the words I'd just spoken.

I thought I needed you.

I stared at CNN and waited for the inevitable.

The kid was quiet in my room.

My hand rubbed the scar beneath my eyebrow.

I thought I needed you.

Chapter 28:
Family Rules - Part VIII

It was the first time that Jamie and Chris had argued on camera. The first time that on-screen tension had risen higher than a set-up for some inevitable, telegraphed punch-line. It was the final season of *Family Rules!* though none of us knew that for certain. The popularity of the show had been waning; format and cast tired, losing their power to pull in the audience every week.

Sure, Jamie was still the number one girl-next-door but somehow all the jokes in the world couldn't make up for the fact that she kept her top on all the time.

And Chris had filled out, his middle as wide as his chest, a suggestion of a double chin that had been growing for too long.

Sanderson.

I avoided Sanderson. It would take years, and my own miserable dive into avoidance, to realise that the bottom of a bottle is a lonely, desperate place.

So Jamie and Chris fought, in the Producer's vain attempt to regain some viewers by ripping my family apart.

Joel treated the shoot as if it were a movie aimed at the Oscars; a bull in this room of porcelain egos, raging from one actor to the other.

"Your lines, Chris... Do you know your lines?"

Receiving blank indifference.

"Sure, I get it... I know what you're up to, you jacked up little ponce. Well you can just come down off that high horse right now... We're still paying your fucking rent and that movie deal hasn't come through yet, so you don't want to start burning your bridges too soon, you never... Jamie!"

He span, roaring over to her. I sat and watched it all – my head turning like a tennis fan at Wimbledon. Somehow, mainly thanks to my age, I'd managed to avoid these tirades so far, my acting coach and minders bearing most of the brunt.

And that was when it happened.

Jamie spoke up.

"Joel," the calmness in her voice drew our attention.

He continued striding over towards her.

"Joel."

And this time he stopped, sensing the cobra coiled in her voice, readying to strike. He stared at her, silent.

"Listen to me," she said, "and listen carefully. You are going to stop this. You are going to stop all the shouting and swearing and bullying and criticism and bullshit that you keep throwing at us."

He looked like someone had torn off his fingernails and doused them with salt. A noise began in the back of his throat that may have been a word or a scream; whatever it was, it rapidly grew towards apoplexy.

"No Joel," Jamie continued, implacable, standing from where she'd sat reading her lines, "you can just stop that. It's not going to work. You act like a five year-old. Your tantrums are over."

She gestured towards me without breaking eye contact with our Director.

"Kenny has more dignity than you've ever had. You could learn something from him."

In that moment, I basked in the glow. Her words meant nothing, her gesture, her inclusion of me, everything. Her hand dropped to her side as she walked towards him.

"This show is going to hell in a hand-cart and we all know it. The game is almost over. We all are. So it's time you started acting like we all feel. We're earning money now, delivering to our contracts and no amount of huffing, puffing and trying to blow the house in is going to make the slightest bit of difference to any of us. We are all out of a job at the end of this season, yourself included, so get your head straight and get off our backs."

Everyone was staring at her. Staring. Like you'd stare at a tiger if it just happened to walk into the room.

Joel, ever the preening ego, didn't seem to have heard a word of it. His face reddened, veins beginning to stand out alongside tendons in his neck. His eyes flared. His mouth opened and...

"No, Joel. It's time for you to say *nothing*."

She lifted her arm and her hand fell on his chest. She didn't even look like she was trying.

"There was a time when you had the right to treat us like a bunch of kids. You had that right – we were crap, we were learning, *I* was learning. But not any more, Joel. Not any more."

She smiled now and sadness washed her face.

"We're on the good ship Titanic, my friend. So wake up."

"But..." Joel squeaked.

"But what?" Jamie fired back. "Are you really so wrapped up in your little world that you can't even work out that it's over. Jesus, Joel! There was a time when you were like a father to us all. When you took us in hand. When you pointed us right. When you... When you loved us! Despite all the dramatics and tantrums, I knew you loved us. But you lost it, Joel. You lost it years ago. Somehow, this show, this little world where you're king of all you survey, somehow that became more important than me, Chris, Kenny and all the others."

Out of the corner of my eye, I noticed Sanderson wince when she didn't name him; ego pricked.

"When did it happen, Joel? Huh? Was it when we got nominated for that first award? The second? Was it the article in Radio Times? Or the centre spread in the Sunday Times magazine? Because the truth is, Joel, that this thing has been going downhill since then. Since you stopped caring about us."

There was a tear in Jamie's eye; her hand still on his chest, resting with little pressure.

"You were like a father to me, Joel. Like a father. And I don't think you even knew. I learned everything from you. Everything. But not like this. Not this shouting. Not this bullying madness. There was a time…"

Her hand dropped from his chest.

"I thought I needed you."

A moment of silence. We all stared at something that wasn't Jamie and Joel; a piece of fluff on the carpet, or a drink stain on the coffee table, or the way the lights cast little shadows across the set, anything but Jamie and Joel.

"Now though," Jamie hissed quietly, "you can just go and fuck yourself. Let's get to work."

She walked off towards the set.

Leaving us looking at whatever had suddenly become so interesting.

Chris blew a little sigh out through closed lips. It sounded like he was whistling.

Joel just stood there, looking at the empty space that had held Jamie. Energy radiated from him; vibrating. Jaw clenched, veins almost bursting.

Without a word, his hand dropped to his side and picked up a vase from where it sat on the coffee table. Silent, he hurled it against the wall where it exploded into fragments; water spattered an epicentre on the wallpaper.

"Bitch!" he hissed.

He kicked the coffee table.

Chris and Martin stared at the spectacle, ready to look away the moment Joel chose to look at them.

"I made her!" Joel was raging, kicking the table to punctuate each word. "She was nothing! Just some fucking tart with a good set of tits that they wanted to get on the box! I made her everything she is! Everything! Who the fuck does she think she is?"

I wanted this to stop. I wanted him to stop. It was too scary. Too scary.

"Joel," I said quietly.

He didn't hear me. His hand rested on a chair to his side.

"... Jumped up little cow. *I thought I needed you? I thought I needed you!* She might as well go back to flashing her tits in the newspaper... Not as if she's got any talent to go on and do anything else, is it? She should just go and fuck the..."

"Joel," I spoke a bit louder.

And he turned now, hurling the chair in sheer, inarticulate rage; no words, no direction, no intent, just an explosion of anger.

The chair flew through the air. I watched it all the way.

As it came directly at me.

I saw the air it displaced.

And then it hit me in the face, knocking me backwards onto the floor, where I lay, tasting blood in my mouth, seeing red as blood flowed, filling my eyes.

I thought I needed you, Jamie's words the last to go through my head.

I passed out.

Chapter 29:
In for a Penny

The doorbell rang. It took a moment for me to surface from my stupor; CNN ticker, a hypnotist's watch.

The kid was sitting on the floor, playing with some cards I'd found in a draw. She dropped them, picked them up, dropped them, picked them up. No particular rhyme or reason, no method or rule-set.

She looked as bored as I was.

The doorbell rang again. Twice.

I walked down the hallway, looking over my shoulder to check the kid hadn't followed me, and then looked through the spyhole.

And saw Ivvy on the other side.

I recoiled from the door, heartbeat racing, until my back slammed against the far wall.

How had she got up here? Why hadn't the doorman called up?

I fought my breath into control.

She rang the doorbell.

Knew I was in the apartment.

She used her badge, paranoia flashed a neon thought, *she knows what I've done and she used her badge to get past the doorman.*

And if she'd used her badge, then she was here as a cop, not as a friend. And that meant I couldn't let her in. No way.

She rang the doorbell again and I heard her voice this time.

"Ken?"

Muffled by the security door.

I slid down the wall until I was sitting.

"Ken?"

* * *

A couple of seconds later, my cellphone trilled into life.

I answered it on autopilot.

"Ken," she said, "open the door."

"Ken?"

"Ivvy."

"Open the door."

"Ivvy, why are you here?"

"Just open the goddamned door!"

I stood and unbolted the door, letting it loose in the frame. It came towards me slowly as she pushed it open.

Here she was, revealed, crossing the hall towards me and I was powerless to do anything but watch, knowing that the game was up, that she was going to find the kid and that would be that for me.

But she was walking up to me, opening her arms, pulling me into a hug and resting her head on my shoulder. I felt her breath on my neck. And a wetness; tears.

"I'm sorry," she mumbled into my shoulder.

Now she pulled back.

"I'm sorry, all right? I didn't…"

Now she looked at me.

"What?"

"Ivvy," I said, confused, "why are you here?"

She breathed. Stared at me.

"Ivvy?"

She looked behind her, saw the open door, closed it. We were alone in the hallway; sound of CNN drifting through from the living room.

Ivvy stared at me. Hard.

"Last night we…"

There was no we last night, I thought, there was just me, kidnapping a child by accident.

"We shouldn't have left it like that. You were… And then the call this morning. You were so conf… Are you all right?"

No, Ivvy, I'm not.

"Yeah, I'm fine. Just got a bit freaked out by that book, you know?"

She shook her head and there was a metallic glint to her eyes.

"Don't start that bullshit again. It wasn't just the book. I heard you this morning. I heard you."

She was staring at me and I knew that this wasn't one of Ivvy's typical interrogations. This time it was for real.

I was tired. Too tired for the game.

Which was about to be officially *up*.

"Come on," I said and turned towards the living room.

I heard her sling her purse down on the bench just inside the doorway, kicking off her shoes, and then the soft padding of her footfalls behind mine.

As we entered the room, the kid looked up.

"Ivvy," I said, "I'm a daddy."

* * *

For a second we stood, the two of us, framed in the doorway, staring at the kid. I was conscious of the television in the background; the sun glancing off windows a couple of blocks away. Ivvy tried to compute what I'd just said and what was sitting on the floor playing with the cards. I could feel my breath rasping in my throat, the ache in my arms from carrying the kid across Manhattan, a headache beginning to form behind my eyes.

And the kid played on with its cards, only glancing up for a moment to see who had stepped into the room.

A moment, captured in reflected sunlight.

* * *

I expected questions. I expected lots of questions.

But what I got was Ivvy turning on her heel and walking into the kitchen.

I followed her.

But stopped just as I was about to step out of the living room. I turned, walked back to the kid and crouched down. The kid looked up at me. Smiled a little.

"What's your name?" I whispered.

The kid didn't answer.

"What is your name?"

There was a glint in its eyes; sensing a game?

"No," I said, "no games. Tell me your name."

My fingers touched my chest and I nodded.

"I'm Ken," I said.

I reached out to touch the kid's chest, making it squirm. Nothing in response.

I touched my chest again.

"Ken," I said, growing more conscious that Ivvy was still out in the kitchen.

I touched the kid again.

"Bella," she said quietly.

"Bella?"

"Uh-huh."

I almost felt like shaking her hand with a formal *good morning* or something. But the name was good enough for now.

Good enough for what I'd got planned.

I stood and walked through to the kitchen.

*   *   *

The kettle was roaring.

Ivvy ground some coffee beans for the French press that sat on the counter next to the cups.

She didn't speak.

I leant against the counter, thoughts whirring.

I didn't speak.

*   *   *

As she handed me a mug of coffee, I broke the silence.

"Jamie," I said.

She just stared at me.

I knew no more of what was coming next than she did; the path begun, I had no choice but to follow.

"A couple of years back, I had a… I was with a girl called Jamie. Didn't last long. "

Ivvy frowned a little.

"It was just as you and I were getting to know each other," I said, trying to ease that frown, "and it was over so quickly that I never thought to mention it. Didn't really mean anything. She was a student, only in the city for one semester. To tell the truth, I'd all but forgotten her."

Ivvy stared at me, her gaze diving into my eyes on a mission to uncover a lie.

"What?" I asked, conscious that I was out on a precipice, precarious above the chasm.

"What does she look like?" Ivvy asked, and it wasn't mere interest driving her question; her day job, I couldn't forget her day job.

Fortunately, I had a template from which to answer her question. So I wasn't forced on the defensive, not then.

"Huh? What's that got to do with anything?"

"I just wanted to know, that's all."

She eased back a little.

"Why? Are you jealous?"

"Fuck you."

"Sorry," I said, "this morning has been a bit weird, all right?"

She nodded.

"Jamie looks just like Bella, okay?"

"Just like Bella."

*   *   *

I might as well have been staring into a camera.

Reading a script.

Living an invented life.

I could play this role.

* * *

"So, she just turns up here this morning, buzzes me from downstairs, asks me to come down to the lobby."

"When I get down there, she's nowhere to be seen, though. And Bella was just standing there with the doorman. He tells me that Jamie wants me to look after Bella for a moment, that she'll be right back."

"So I bring Bella up here, get her settled and everything and then wait for Jamie. But she doesn't come back. A couple of minutes later, she calls me. Must've been watching to check I'd picked up Bella and brought her upstairs."

This was now what had happened; speaking it had made it real. I could play this role.

I shook my head a little, recalling an imagined conversation.

"And she just lays it out there and then. That she'd got pregnant while we were together, hadn't told me at the time, kept the baby but now she needed some time and that I'd have to look after Bella while she got her shit together."

"*Congratulations, Dad.* That's what she said and then she put the phone down. Just like that."

I shook my head again.

* * *

Ivvy stared at me for a long time.

* * *

We stood saying nothing, thinking everything, Bella began to cry a little through in the living room. Ivvy and I stared at each other, each willing the other to do something about it. But then I remembered, I was the Dad in this scene.

I walked through to Bella and crouched down. She was staring at the cards, crying softly.

"Bella," I said, hearing my voice soften, "what's wrong?"

She didn't answer.

"Bella."

My hand reached out slowly, on autopilot, and I watched as it reached beneath Bella's chin, turning her head to look at me. Tears were beginning to mark her cheeks.

"What's wrong?"

I wracked my brain to try and work it out. Whatever it was, Bella wasn't telling.

On my back, Ivvy's gaze was heavy. I still felt like I was being judged, my every move a potential pitfall.

Bella had brown eyes.

Mine are blue.

"C'mon Bella, what's wrong?"

"Bekphust," she said in a small voice, slurred by tears.

"Huh?"

"She wants some breakfast, stupid!" Ivvy said, chuckling a little, "strike one, Daddy!"

And with that, Ivvy abandoned the inquisition, turning on her heel to walk back through to the kitchen.

"Are you hungry?" I asked Bella.

She nodded solemnly.

"Want some breakfast?"

Again a nod.

"C'mon then," I said and offered my hand to pull her up. She jumped into my arms, just as she had the previous night, when I'd opened the car door on Riverside Drive. She clung to my neck.

My autopilot hand stroked her back, calming her down as I stood.

When I looked toward the kitchen, Ivvy was standing in the doorway, watching me, wearing a smile that I'd never seen before. It softened her face.

"What?" I asked.

"You... Oh nothing," she waved a dismissive hand and turned back into the kitchen.

I carried Bella out of the living room.

I was the role I had cast for myself: *Man who learns he's a father.*

I was *Kramer vs Kramer.*

I was *Three Men and a Baby.*

I was in deep shit but had no other way out than the one I'd chosen.

I could play this role.

I was carrying my daughter.

I was moving forward.

Chapter 30:
Family Rules – Part IX

"Who nicked my fags?" Chris raged into the cafeteria.

Seventeen heads swivelled to face him, unused to such an outburst. If it had been Martin or Joel, I doubt anyone would have done more than glance; their tantrums as regular and indispensable as breathing. To them at least. But Chris rarely raised his voice above a level more suitable for pleasant conversation, mostly only getting louder when the script absolutely demanded it.

So, we sat and stared. Jamie to my left, my minder to the right, Sanderson opposite. And Joel? Joel didn't eat with us by then. Not since Jamie's assertion and reclamation of control. Joel was *otherwise engaged* unless he was filming, when the old, vituperative Joel would once again stalk the sets, throwing tantrums and criticism with vicious disdain.

"Chris?" Jamie asked, breaking the tableau out of its freeze. Others went back to whatever discussion or mouthful they'd been chewing over.

Chris walked over to our table and sat down on the bench next to Sanderson.

"I went back to my dressing room and someone's been in there," he explained, nonplussed, anger only sub-dermal. "My bag's been turned out and all my stuff's on the bed."

Jamie breathed in quickly, a classic intake of breath.

"Was anything stolen?" she asked, near incredulous.

"I just said, didn't I?" Chris fired back. "Someone nicked my ciggies."

"Yeah, I heard you," Jamie continued, "but I meant anything important."

"Huh?"

"Like money or something."

"No," Chris shook his head, "but that isn't the point. Someone's been in there and been through my gear and turned it over. The only thing that's missing is a pack of cigarettes as far as I can tell. What sort of bastard would do that?"

He turned his head slightly, looked at Sanderson out the corner of his eye. Remained silent just long enough for the older man to pick up on the energy.

"What?" Sanderson said.

"You got any cigarettes on you?" Chris asked, suspicion coiled in his words.

"I..." Sanderson replied, "er... No, actually, I don't. Maybe Jamie... er...Jamie?"

He looked across the table at the star of the show and shrugged.

"Chris?" Jamie asked and waited until the younger man looked at her. "What are you doing?"

Chris looked at her for a long time. And then shook his head.

"Nothing," he said, voice resigned to defeat, "it just pisses me off, that's all. It's not the fags. Christ! It's only a couple of quid. It's the principle of the thing, you know. I would have..."

I reached up and put the cigarette pack on the table, quietly, hoping that no-one would notice.

Some hope.

"Kenny?" Sanderson blurted out, deciding to out me in the most obvious way.

"Huh?" Chris looked up, looked across the table at me.

"Huh?" Jamie turned her head to look at me.

Chris stared at the cigarette pack.

Jamie stared at the cigarette pack.

I tasted cigarettes, burnt in my mouth and making the back of my throat ache.

Then Chris went ballistic.

Chapter 31:
Walk in the Park

Ivvy watched Bella while I showered and got dressed. Pretty soon though, it was time for her to go to work. Bella and I gave her a hug goodbye and waved her off; perfect family kicking off another perfect day.

We closed the door on Ivvy.

The tension flooded out of me so fast and hard that I could have cried. It shuddered through me, shredding my breath, sending my heart racing.

Head bowed, tremors shimmered up and down my body, hairs stood to attention along my forearms. Tears pricked my eyes. A lump in my throat that I couldn't swallow past.

I sobbed. Once. Loud and clear and then covered my mouth with my hand, trying to hold it back, to stifle the burgeoning panic.

Eyes clenched shut, I fought not to think about what had just happened. What was happening right now. But the darkness was far more terrible than anything I could have looked at; it held demons. So I opened my eyes and there stood Bella. No halo, no ring of reflected sunlight, no angelic choirs. Just Bella, standing in the hallway of my parents' apartment, that house of desolation, home to no-one. She looked at me, expression blank. Bottom lip pouting a little but nowhere near tears. Frightened, most definitely. It was in her eyes; all wariness and staring.

"It's OK, Bella," I whispered, my voice tremulous, "it's OK."

"It's going to be OK."

Me, the target of the reassurance; hollow promise.

I walked past Bella, through to the living room, sat on the couch unable to move, staring blankly at CNN.

Still nothing.

Nothing.

* * *

Finally, enough was enough.

I couldn't sit in the apartment anymore, couldn't sit and watch CNN cycle through the same piece of news, analysis and conjecture for another minute. Couldn't listen to the *flick, flack* of the playing cards to which Bella had returned.

"Bella," I said, "do you want to go out for a walk in the park?"

She looked at me, smiled slightly, no more than a twitch at the corners of her mouth, and said, "OK."

We went out to the Park.

* * *

Central Park.

Its quietness dulled the energy of the city to a numbing throb.

Bella and I walked hand in hand into the park, past joggers and strollers and skaters and cyclists and fast-food uniforms and families and tourists. All of them enjoying this audacious simulacrum of nature.

Bella laughed as some squirrels ran up and down trees, fighting over acorns.

A rat ran through the undergrowth.

Bella laughed.

*   *   *

We sat in Sheep Meadow for a while, its broad sweep of grass calm beneath frisbees, soccer balls, baseballs, footballs. Couples lay on the grass, in each others' arms. Acoustic guitars were strummed like it was the sixties again. Only it wasn't; *'Green Day'* and *'Nirvana'* substituting for *'The Mamas and Papas'*.

I couldn't help but scan the grass for cops. None to be seen. They would have been patrolling the roadways on bikes and little golf buggies, calling off joggers and in-line skaters.

I suddenly wondered which day of the week it was.

Saturday, I thought, *it must be Saturday.*

Bella's mother had been going home from work when I'd stolen her car; dressed for the office.

The previous night had been Friday.

The weekend; New Yorkers out in force in the park.

Could only have been Saturday.

Bella picked at the grass.

I looked at her. Scanned for cops.

I had this role to play, this daughter. What did I do next? This role. What did a single father do in the city when he had his kid for the Saturday?

He...

He...

Went and bought some clothes because Bella was still wearing the gear she'd had on when I kidnapped her. So much for scanning for cops. Bella was a walking billboard, yelling loud and clear that here she was. Always on the news, it was the same line: *"Last seen wearing..."*, and I'd always thought to myself that the first thing anyone was going to do when they wanted to disappear was get changed, put on some different clothes.

Like my hip-hop disguise.

Here I was bringing Bella out into the park dressed fully in the same clothes that those news reports would be describing to the most exact details. What had I been thinking?

"Bella," I spoke and she looked up from the grass, "I…"

"Yeah?" she said and in a split second, I wanted to explain everything that had happened since I'd done my gangsta stereotype across the gas station forecourt, hopped into their car and driven away. I wanted to explain that I didn't mean her any harm, that I really, really wanted to go back a day but I couldn't and I couldn't because I didn't want to get in trouble. I didn't want to get in trouble. I didn't want…

*　*　*

Over to the Upper West, away from the apartment. If I was spotted, I didn't want it to be in my home neighbourhood. Besides, I knew that there would be some kids' shops there.

My intuition paid off.

There were kids' shops, all right, loads of them. Everything from national chains to little Mom and Pop outfits. It made my stomach ache with anxiety for about two minutes trying to decide which was least likely to pay me any undue attention, knowing that they would all have security cameras, that I was going to be caught on tape no matter what. How to do that without drawing attention to myself? How to…

In the end, I just walked straight into Gap, grabbed a couple of handfuls of clothes, estimating Bella's size, and paid for them. As quick and as easily as I could; a stressed father unused to buying clothes for his kid and eager to be somewhere else. When I came to pay, I mumbled something about her mother being out-of-town and my having appointments; something hasty, something improvised. All the time I watched to see whether anyone paid too much attention to Bella. Aside from a little smile in her direction, that Bella naturally reciprocated, the shop assistants seemed more focused on counting down their shift.

From Gap, I walked a couple of blocks holding Bella's hand, found a packed bar and stepped inside, cutting straight through to the restrooms, got inside, got Bella changed out of her clothes and into one of the dresses.

Flashback to a bloodied shirt.

To a burning can on the lower East.

Adrenalin fired again – I was growing accustomed to its rush.

Did I ditch Bella's clothes here or somewhere else. The apartment? In the park? Could someone find them and trace them back?

Too many questions and an inevitable conclusion.

There was no way I could second guess the future. No way I could prevent what might happen, whatever it may be.

I could only act my role.

I stuffed her clothes in the Gap bag, deciding to ditch them in a trashcan in the park.

All the time, Bella was quiet, smiling every so often and keeping herself to herself.

Which was good because it gave me time to wonder what I was going to do next.

The park was a great option. Safety in numbers. And now that Bella was no longer a billboard, I guessed I could rest easier there.

But I had this role to play.

And I had a child to entertain.

What the hell did a parent do with a kid in New York?

*   *   *

We sat and watched weekend warriors feed bread to the ducks. On the lake in front of us, couples paddled by in rented boats, noisy teenagers courting and daring each other who could lean furthest out of the boat.

You don't want to drop in the water, I thought, *not knowing how many rats live in the park.*

Bella pointed at the ducks and laughed. I watched the ornate bridge over the boating lake for police.

Joggers ran past on the path, shedding pounds, filling their lungs with all the particulates that float in New York's smog.

Beyond the bridge, *The Rambles*, its square mile of undergrowth and twisted paths, the wildest place in the city; fun to walk in, an imagined forest.

My cell phone rang.

Ivvy's number.

"Yeah?"

"Where are you?"

"The Park. Boating Lake."

"Near The Rambles?"

"Uh-huh."

"You staying around?"

I twitched at the question, that morning's paranoia kicking in again from where it had been lurking all the time, just below the surface.

"I might be," I said, trying to sound casual, but just sounding guilty, "why?"

"I'm almost done for the day, thought I'd come and join you."

"Caught any good Johns lately?" My anxiety put a bite in the words.

"Fuck you," she laughed at the other end, easing me down.

"And the horse you rode in on," I fired back.

"Well," she asked, "are you hanging around there or do you want to meet me at your place?"

That made me think. Did I want her to come over? Did I want to spend any more time than necessary with her and Bella together?

But I was playing this role, I was a father. I had no choice. I couldn't ditch the kid. Could I? No. I was a dad now. And Ivvy wanted to play happy families. And for all I knew, Bella's photo was by then playing on every news channel across the city, people sitting in bars watching the news, people in shopping malls seeing Bella's photograph tessellated across a hundred TV screens, Times Square streaming her picture, all marching in synchronicity.

I could just give her to the police, I thought.

She laughed again at the ducks.

Got up to walk towards them.

"Where are you?" I asked Ivvy.

"SoHo," she said, "just down from the Apple store."

"What... Ready to leave now?"

"Just about," she said.

"Well, we're probably going to..."

A cop was walking across the bridge, suspended above squabbling teenagers and ravenous ducks.

"... uh... be here for about a half hour. Can you get here by then?"

The cop got to the near end of the bridge, stopped, looked around, spoke into the radio clipped to his lapel.

"Yeah, if I get a cab!" Ivvy sounded pissed off now. "Can't you give me a little while longer? I just want to spend some time with you and Bella."

The cop looked right at me.

"You just want to play happy families, right?" I hissed into the phone.

The cop stared at me. Sunlight glinting off his sunglasses. Looking straight at me.

"You are such an asshole," Ivvy snapped back and I remembered what I'd just said, "I'll be there as soon as I can. Don't go anywhere."

She ended the call and I put the phone back in my pocket.

The cop was staring right at me and as I looked back at him, I grew aware of a great noise behind me, of squealing and screaming and moving bodies and I just automatically thought of Bella, of where...

Bella!

I couldn't see her.

I heard the splash of bodies in the water and was on my feet and looking and hearing the screaming and shouting and seeing the cop, looking in my direction but beginning to run, to run in my direction and I was thinking that the game was up and where the fuck was Bella and I couldn't see her and the cop was running. I span in circles, looking in all directions, seeing people look at me, past me, through me and I couldn't see the child but everyone was moving towards the lake and the cop was running and speaking into the radio at his shoulder and I was still spinning but Bella was nowhere and nowhere and nowhere and my eyes were going red with the sun and the heat and where was Bella and...

I woke up flat on my back, staring at the sun. No crowd had gathered around me. No time had elapsed. The noise was still going on but it was by the water's edge now and I wondered if they'd found her tiny body floating on its surface, dead because her new father couldn't even keep an eye on her during a two minute phone call.

I hadn't been ready to be a father.

But I'd had no choice.

I started walking towards the scene, seeing stars and blood pressure specks dance before my eyes, tears beginning to form.

The cop was at the water's edge and as I drew near, staying towards the back of the crowd in case I needed to make a quick exit, I heard him talking into his radio.

"... right, there's just two of them. I'll bring them in."

Stepping out of the lake, looking guilty and embarrassed but still unable to keep the grins from their faces, were a man and a younger – a much younger – woman; him about fifty and her in her early twenties. Both of them naked. He wasn't doing so well with his years, she was yet to feel the gravitational tug of hers. He gave her a round of applause, politely, nodding his approval. She returned the compliment.

The cop got hold of them both and asked them where their clothes are.

The man pointed up the hill, to where they'd discarded them during their mad dash into the boating lake.

"Get dressed," the cop tried to stay serious but even he was picking up on the infectious energy these two gave off. As were the crowd, laughing each time they laughed.

The love between these two was unmistakable.

They walked up the hill, followed by the cop, crowd parting before them like a field of corn.

Before they got to their clothes, they had linked arms and, aside from their nudity, could have been any couple out for a stroll in the park.

The cop fought hard not to look at her ass.

Me? I drank it in. Slightly embarrassed but still warm and fuzzy.

Watching her walk up the hill, in the company of the man she loved, the crowd dispersing around me, happy to feel the warmth again, the paranoia easing off because...

The jolt was severe.

Like electricity. Adrenalin surged through me, clenching my teeth hard.

I bit my tongue.

Bella was nowhere to be seen.

Nowhere.

I stood, looking around me.

Nowhere.

Not on the grass, nor in the water.

Nowhere.

Nowhere.

*   *   *

A wave of scotch breezed Sanderson into the trailer.

I sat and looked at the table. At the cards. At my fingernails. My five year old fingernails.

Whorls, knots in the veneer of the table top. Plastic detailing, a pretence to life.

Five years old.

He crossed to sit at my side.

*   *   *

I stared at the sky above the lakeside. Seeking divine inspiration or oblivion or a bit of both.

Wishing lightning would strike me.

Right now.

Knowing that this was an opportunity, as much as it was panic.

I could walk.

I could turn around and act like the kid hadn't ever been a part of my life.

There. Then. Me.

I stared at blue sky rendered through the city's heat haze and smog; humidity and acid rain in waiting.

My eyes burned. Close to tears. Watching the blue above me.

Knowing that there were teeth. That there were hunters.

That there were predators.

Knowing that I could walk away.

Wishing I could walk away.

Predators.

Chapter 32:
Family Rules – Part X

When he exhaled, the stench of whisky redoubled.

The table top. The cards. My fingernails.

"How are you, Kenny?" Slight slurring.

I didn't speak.

Sanderson didn't say anything. For a long time.

Glancing out the corner of my eye; his eyes closed. I turned my head, pretty sure that he was out, passed out. I looked at him. He snorted in his sleep, half-snore, half-choke, and I thought he was coming back.

But he didn't.

And I counted my blessings.

Closed my eyes.

Counted my blessings.

Tried to work out just how I was going to get out from behind the table when he was right in the way, when his feet were spread out beneath the table. When the only route out was to step over his legs.

The only escape.

My own legs too short to be able to step over without touching him.

I opened my eyes. Looked at him. Listened to the rhythm of his snoring.

Finally, I got up the confidence to stand.

Stood for a while, watching and listening – remembering the morning when my father had roared at me in their bed, when I had run to hide in the gap between my own bed and the wall. Not knowing what it was about Sanderson that scared me, a fear that had been building for a long time, some intuitive part of me sensing something in him.

The only way to get out was to turn my back on him, leaning away, lifting my left leg and stepping sideways, like a clown accentuating every movement. Me straddling his legs, half-crouching, half-sitting, furiously listening for any change in his breathing. Waiting a long, long time. No change in his breathing, that rumbling snore; in and out, rumble and rattle. Steadying myself to lift my right foot, to complete the manoeuvre. Off balance, I began to fall, catching myself early enough to stay silent and standing.

His hand on my neck was like a vice; sudden, excruciating.

"Where the fuck do you think you're going?" he roared. His voice drunken, loud and crowing, as if he were performing to a theatre auditorium.

I didn't say a thing.

He yanked me backwards, lifting me off my feet and I was cocooned in his scotch breath and old man's arms, sitting on his lap, unable to squirm, his free arm snaking around me and pinioning me to his chest.

"Don't you move!" he hissed, spit speckling my ear and cheek.

My five year old ear and cheek.

I stopped trying to struggle; the noise that escaped me was the whimpering of a starved puppy crying for food or its mother's teat.

"Shut up."

I couldn't.

"Shut up," his hand grabbed my ear and twisted hard.

"Quite the prima donna, aren't you little Kenny?" he spat, "got every one of them wrapped around your cutesy, cutesy little finger. Especially that bitch Jamie, especially her."

He tensed as he spoke her name, tensed against me.

"Bitch!"

He was quiet for a moment. Then he started to mumble under his breath. Words slipping through.

"Bring her down a peg or two... make her... bitch... who does she think..."

"Stand up," he said.

I did so, still straddling his legs, which he now opened, placing them either side of me, pinning me between his thighs. I began to turn around, to look at him but he stopped me with his hand on the back of my shoulder.

"No," he said, "keep facing that way."

I stared at the wall on the other side of the table.

Wondered where my minder was. For the first time in this whole extended moment, wondering where she was.

He snuffled behind me, grunting, panting. Hissing under his breath. Words. Disconnected and bilious.

Where was she?

His grunts.

Where?

I sprinted for the door, tripping over his legs, kicking out to get clear, sprawling on the floor, dreading the feel of his claw on my neck again. When I glanced back, he was doubled over on the seat, head between his knees, breathing hard. I jumped to my feet and ran for the door.

Just to find it opening, Jamie pushing it towards me.

I dashed into her arms. Beginning to sob without realizing it was starting.

She held me for a moment and then looked over my shoulder.

"Martin?"

"Fuck off," he hissed, head still between his knees, looking at the ground.

"What did you do, Kenny?" she asked.

And I couldn't speak.

"Martin?"

Nothing.

"What did you do, Kenny?" More forceful this time. Accusing me.

The sound of his fly going up was crystal clear. The sound of him getting to his feet, putting himself away, the rattle of his zip.

I began to panic, thinking that it wasn't over. That she wasn't the saviour I'd called for while he'd done whatever he did behind my back.

She took a step backward through the door, out of the trailer.

She's going to leave me with him, I thought.

"Don't leave me, Jamie!" I screamed.

"Yeah, right," she said, laughing a little, "like *that's* gonna happen!"

And he roared.

She carried me straight to Joel's trailer.

Where she spilled everything.

As I sat listening to stuff that I didn't have a hope of understanding, I worshipped her. I worshipped her force, her strength, her beauty. And I worshipped Joel's reaction.

The last thing I saw before she whisked me away was Joel dragging Sanderson out of the trailer by his hair.

Chapter 33: Saviour

I ran to the water's edge, looked at the muddy surface; algae and turbulence.

Nothing. Nothing. Nothing.

Turned back, looked up the hill at the waiting masses, deflated after their midsummer madness spectacle; back to sitting on the grass and waiting to die.

Nothing.

Looked right, towards the Dakota building rising over the trees of Strawberry Fields.

Nothing.

Children, yes. Holding their parents' hands, bouncing balls, playing with dogs, licking ice creams, teetering on roller blades. All of that.

But sign of Bella? Nothing.

I looked the other way, where the path wound to the ornamental bridge, The Rambles on the other side, rising rocks and thickening undergrowth.

I knew in my gut that she'd gone in there.

That intuition, a niggle that made me feel like I wanted to crap or puke or both at the same time.

If I'd been a parent, I would have gone straight to the nearest cop.

Only, at that moment, I didn't know whether I would have asked him to help me find Bella or just handed myself in.

I wanted to be her father.

I wanted it more than anything.

I didn't want to be alone with the panic. With the threat.

I headed towards the bridge, fighting back the urge to run, biting down on the panic as it rose like a lava burst. Up the steps, onto the bridge and crossing its smooth wooden surface, looking ahead, left, right, seeing nothing, no sign of her nor a glimpse of her new clothes amongst the throngs.

Into The Rambles.

Wilderness New York style; contrived, manufactured, designed and yet somehow just the right side of being farcical. Paths crumbled through neglect, steps cracked and broken, small rivulets of water found their own way down the mini-escarpment at the centre of the wilderness.

I tried to imagine where she might have gone. She was only small, so climbing the steps was out unless... No. I would not consider that somebody had snatched her. No.

No.

I followed the path around by the side of the lake. Trees and undergrowth grew thicker as I advanced, the sound of the city summer fading as I left the rowing boats behind.

I heard her crying.

As the sound of the crowd back at the lake diminished, I heard her crying.

How I knew it was her, I didn't know.

I began to run.

And saw her through the trees at the intersection of two paths, standing, crying. With a bum towering over her. She was looking up at him, terrified, and I didn't know what he had done; was doing. I began to run harder, finding no voice to shout. No voice. I wanted to scream. I wanted to scream at him to get away from her.

From my daughter.

But nothing came out.

I thought of Sanderson, being dragged across the lot by Joel, his hair stretching out above his head.

I was closing in.

"Bella!" I yelled, finally finding my voice.

She didn't hear me, just stayed staring up at the bum.

I could smell him now, coming closer, within range, hoping I wasn't too late.

He didn't hear me.

He crouched by her side. Spoke to her.

Reached out a hand, put it under her chin, turned her face to his, leaned in as if to kiss her and I hit him like a train; no grace, no tackle, no form, I just ran straight into him. He fell with me and we tumbled in a tumult of limbs, over and around each other.

When we stopped moving, I opened my eyes and was looking at the ground.

"What the fuck?" the bum shouted, his voice shredded by too many years on the street, *"what are you doing, man?"*

And then he was on my back, his hands, scabby, crusted, reaching around to claw at my eyes. I smelled his breath as it wafted around my head, enveloping me, a cloud that tightened my throat and choked my own breath.

"Stop it!" I yelled, but his fingers continued to scrabble at my cheek, skittering like cockroaches, clawing like talons. As I thrashed to avoid their grasp, I caught sight of Bella and she wasn't just crying any more, she was screaming her lungs out, horrified by what she was witnessing.

Seeing her there, knowing she was watching, that she was seeing me pinned by this bum who was in the act of...

I thrashed harder and succeeded in flipping him off for a moment.

Others were running now, drawn by Bella's screams.

Double the entertainment today, an illogical thought flashed through my head.

The bum was on his feet and coming at me again. I stayed on my knees and as he drew near enough, fired myself upward, shoulder into his gut, lifting him off his feet as I stood, carrying him off his feet. We continued the parabola and I was suddenly dropping through the air towards him as he landed on his back, badly winded. I hit him, full force, jarring impact shuddering through my shoulder and spine. The top of my head connected with his jaw and it snapped shut.

He lay still and, for the briefest moment, I rested on him.

Only a moment. Bella's tears dragged me away.

There was a woman with her now, crouching down next to her and reaching her hand out under Bella's chin, turning the kid's head to face her and drawing close, like she was about to kiss her.

I did a double take. At Bella, at the bum and back again. Crossed to where Bella stood next to the crouching woman. Bella watched me approach and, for a moment, I wondered whether she would scream at me. Wasn't I just an assailant who'd been around her longer than any other at this particular moment?

But Bella didn't scream, or cry.

She reached her arms out to me.

I scooped her up and held her close.

Looked at the woman as she stood.

"Thank you," I whispered, nuzzling into Bella's hair, smelling the wino but also the kid, "thank you."

The woman looked over at the wino. At Bella and I. Back at the wino.

"I didn't hit him that hard," I said, "he'll sleep it off."

"What about the cops?" she asked.

I shook my head.

"I think he was trying to help," I admitted my mistake, "I thought he was about to… But… But… "

She patted my arm.

"It's OK," she said. "Bums. Too many of them in the city since Giuliani left – can't trust them. Are you gonna be OK?"

I nodded.

She smiled. "You'd better get that girl home to her mother. And hey, do me a favour, OK? Buy her an ice cream on the way, OK?"

I smiled a little at this.

The woman looked down at the bum and her distaste was clear. Like she could have spat on him. Like she felt like she should have spat on him. Looked back at me. Smiled.

"You're a good father," she said, "have a great day."

She walked away and I was left hugging Bella who was finally quiet, breathing against me.

I walked over to where the bum lay on the ground. Stood still for a moment, listening. Listening.

He was breathing.

I took Bella out of The Rambles, across the fairy-tale bridge, up the hill and through Sheep Meadow, past the zoo, towards home.

We stopped for an ice cream before we left the park, standing at one of the refreshment carts while the guy dug deep inside to find the particular flavour Bella had pointed at on the sign.

Bella and I. Just a father and daughter out for a day in the park.

Bella, my daughter.

Which made me her father.

We finished our ice creams and went home.

Chapter 34:
Inside the Cat's Eyes

I sat across the table from Norris, staring at the book in front of me, trying to make sense of what I was reading.

A cat and a griffin – half eagle, half lion – on a desert island, with a pirate who looked like a matinee idol or a cowboy, dressed in blue, blond hair blowing in the island breeze, no sign of scars nor wounds, the cutlass attached to his hip little more than for show.

The griffin sat on a rock, watching the blue pirate.

Even though this was a reading book for five-year-olds, it was a feat of mental gymnastics just to make sense of the images, let alone the words. Why was that eagle's head and shoulders on a lion's body? It didn't make sense. Why did the blue pirate look so composed when he was meant to be drunk on rum and sunshine?

"Try again," Norris said, patiently now, an easy interaction that we'd slipped into in the weeks since our first, horrifying introduction.

I put my finger under the words.

"T… h…e… The…"

He nodded approval and encouragement.

"T... r... e... a..." looked up at him, trying to judge whether I was doing good, whether I might be caught out at any moment. His only response was a nod; continue.

"... s... u... r... e... Tree..."

"Treh."

"Treh... Trehzure! Treasure! The treasure." I smiled up at him, filled with success from two words.

He nodded.

"The treasure," he said, "what comes next."

He pointed at the page, tapping it lightly with his long, delicate, bony fingers. I looked at the words there, still feeling the elation of two words successfully spoken.

My eye was continually drawn back to that griffin sitting on the rock, chatting to the cat, watching the blue pirate and his meaningless cutlass.

Norris watched me. Intently. Hard.

I watched words blur before me as tears began to prick my eyes.

The pressure.

I couldn't read. I could not read.

He tapped the page.

I could not read.

His finger lifted, came up to my chin, tilting it to face him. I looked at his glasses; light glinting made it difficult to read any expression or emotion within his eyes.

I was forced to trust his slight, empathetic smile.

"Kenny," he said, "calm down. We have as long as it takes, we're in no rush."

"I don't want to read anyway," I grumbled, "reading's stupid."

This actually stopped him, a frown creasing his forehead for a moment. In the time it took to pucker and fade, I really wished I could see past the reflective lenses of his spectacles. But his frown was gone, passing through like a cloud.

"One day, Kenny," he said, voice of empathy once more, "you will come to realise how wrong that statement is. I hope you can remember this conversation because I swear, it will make you laugh out loud. Now, do you want to tell me..."

"That griffin is..."

"Huh?"

"The griffin," I continued, "he knows that the blue pirate is just pretending. He's told the cat. The cat is laughing but keeping it inside. He doesn't want to upset the pirate."

A pause while he replayed what I had said.

"Why... er... why not?"

"Because the pirate feeds him, keeps him on the blue pirate ship where he can get fed on the ship rats and scraps from the table. That cat, he doesn't want to have to live on the island if the blue pirate leaves him behind, so he doesn't want to upset the blue pirate. No way, no how. He doesn't want to upset the pirate."

"That's what you see in the picture?"

"Uh-huh."

I sat back, concerned that I'd done something wrong, that he was going to break his tranquil mentorship and turn nasty.

"Uh... When did you... Er.... Make all that up?"

I looked at him; my turn to be perplexed.

"What?"

"All that, er..." he looked confused, "all that about the cat and the pirate. About the ship."

I shook my head. "I didn't make it up. It's in the story."

A long look. Searching my eyes.

"Kenny. It's not in the story."

"Yes it is."

I pointed at the page.

"Kenny," his voice gained a little force, "we're on the third page. We know the content we've already read. There simply are not enough words to convey the story you just told."

I looked at him. Confused. "But… But it's in the book."

"Kenny. It is not."

I pointed at the picture, at the cat, perched on the rock, looking at the Griffin.

"What?" Norris said.

I tapped the picture again.

"I don't see anything." He peered at the picture.

"Look in the cat's eyes," I said, my voice choking, "look in its eyes."

I sat back in the chair and began to cry.

He looked at the picture for a long time, unaware that he was trying to understand the nature of an emptiness inside me that could make a cartoon cat speak of motive, duplicity, calculation and odds.

Chapter 35:
Snares

Bella was asleep by eight-thirty. One minute, she was walking around, picking up the cards she'd found earlier, putting them down somewhere else, repeating the cycle over and again until the apartment was scattered with playing cards, and then she'd just laid down flat on the floor, asleep.

I left her for a while so that I could keep on staring at the television, flicking from news channel to news channel, expecting something, some flash, some picture, some headline, some ticker pointing its finger at me and letting me know the game was up. But there was nothing. Nothing.

Nothing.

Aside from here and now, in this apartment, it seemed Bella didn't exist.

A little while later, in a gap within the aural backdrop provided by yet another pretty-boy anchor, I suddenly heard her breathing. It was like I hadn't known she was there at all; not even like realizing I'd forgotten her. Adrenalin surged through my system. I looked down at her prone form. Checked my watch. An hour had gone past.

An hour.

I scooped her up and she didn't bat an eyelid, sleeping through the whole manoeuvre.

I left pretty-boy behind, blathering on with some C-list interviewee about the state of celebrity in Hollywood, as I headed down the corridor towards the bedrooms.

Bella needed a t-shirt and, while one of mine would dwarf her, one of my mother's would likely be a better fit, so I decided to put her to bed in my parents' room.

In their bedroom, I rifled through her drawers, looking for t-shirts, light sweaters, anything that could be used as makeshift pyjamas for Bella. All I turned up was Chanel, Ferragamo and other designers whose names I hadn't heard before. Nothing for my little girl, though. Nothing.

Then I struck pay-dirt.

Like any impression-conscious New Yorker, my mother had the requisite amount of work-out gear – little Nike t-shirts, all lycra and figure hugging. Not that she ever went to the gym, of course. One of these little tops looked about right and I held it up against Bella's sleeping form. It looked about right.

I stripped her, throwing her clothes to the floor, realizing for about the third time that day that she had a wet diaper, which I changed before pulling the t-shirt over her head. It was too big for her, but nowhere near as big as one of mine would have been.

As I laid Bella down in the middle of my parents' bed, I remembered the previous night, when she'd tumbled to the floor. My mother unwittingly came to my rescue again; a mountain of throw cushions at the head of the bed. I arranged them, and the pillows, on either side of Bella, so that she wasn't able to roll straight off the bed.

The telephone rang.

"Shit," I looked at Bella, panicked that she would wake. No chance, she slept straight through the ringing of the phone.

I grabbed the handset off the bedside table and rushed through to the kitchen, certain that it was going to be Ivvy checking up on us both, keen to continue the charade of happy families we'd been playing earlier that morning.

"Shhhhh…" I hissed into the phone, "Bella's…"

"Kenneth?"

My father was the last person I had expected to hear.

For a moment, the world swam in front of my eyes and I went cold all over.

"Ungh…"

"Kenny?" he sounded concerned. "Are you there?"

"Yes, Dad."

"Oh… You sounded… Are you all right?"

"I'm fine, just didn't expect to hear your voice."

There was silence for a moment. I was caught between wanting to avoid small talk and not wanting the silence to drag too long.

"How are things going, Dad?"

"Good," he said, "just… Well, you know… Fine, given the circumstances. Your mother…"

Since when did I care? I thought, walking through to the lounge with the phone in hand, eyeing the news coverage.

Since when did you care?

"… has been… It's been good for her, reconnecting with her family. There's a lot of water under the bridge since she last saw them and…"

I suddenly found I couldn't be bothered. With my father, or the news. It wasn't as if I had to monitor the television religiously, the same talking heads were talking, talking, talking and not one mention of Bella anywhere.

"Dad, why are you calling?"

"Oh…"

Yes, 'oh', I thought.

"We're on our way home, Kenny."

I sat down on the couch. My legs began to quiver.

When I tried to speak, my throat was so dry that no words could claw their way out.

My thoughts scrambled, trying to find purchase on anything that made sense, anything that gave me a route forward.

"Kenny?"

"Sorry, Dad," I said, gaining enough control to put in a stalling tactic, "connection's not so good. When... Er... When are you coming back?"

"Oh... Well, your mother wants to stop off in London on the way through, touch base with some old friends. You know, keep an eye on the old country and I could do with checking in with... Old drinking buddies."

I imagined the leer on his face; old haunts, old flames, old ghosts.

"So when do you think you'll be back?"

"Why," his voice was quick, only half jovial, "are you worried we'll gate-crash your party?"

"Huh?"

"Well... While the cat's away... You know?"

"No," I protested and, all of a sudden it fell across me like a wave: *play the role, just play the role*.

"It's not that, I just want to make sure Oliveria comes in before you get back, get the place clean, you know? You don't want to come back to dirty dishes and my shit all over the place, do you?"

He laughed a little at his end, my make-believe enough to persuade him.

"Tuesday, I think," he said, checking his mental calendar, "hang on a sec..."

The line went quiet for a little while, as he worked his smart-phone.

"Yes," he said, "there's a flight back in the early P.M. on Tuesday, gets us into JFK in the early evening. Should be back in the city by nine, ten at the latest."

"OK," I said, unsure whether I could say much more thanks to my whirling dervish thoughts, "I'll get Oliveria in on Monday."

"Sounds good, listen I've got to go, we're heading down to the bar for a wee night-cap. Do you need the flight details?"

"Not really."

"Yes, sure... Why would you? Not like you'd meet us at the airport, is it?"

There was no humour in this last, no vindictiveness either, it was a statement of fact.

"No, wasn't planning on it."

"OK. Bye, then."

"Yeah," I went to press the button but paused for a moment, "Dad?"

"Yes?"

"We'll.." I caught myself, "I'll... Er... I'll be staying at a friend's place when you get back."

"So?"

"No, I mean staying there."

"Who?"

"You don't know her."

"Her?"

"Yes... She's... A friend. You don't know her."

"Oh... OK. Leave us a number when you go."

And with that he put the phone down at his end, leaving me holding a dead lump of plastic and circuits.

As empty as the gulf between us.

* * *

It took me almost an hour to get up the courage to phone Ivvy.

When I did, I got her answering machine.

After the tone, I left my message.

"Ivvy," I said, all purpose and clear intent, "we're gonna have to stay with you for a few days. My parents are coming home. They'll be here on Tuesday. We'll give you a buzz tomorrow and work out times and all that shit. We need to go shopping for stuff for Bella if you want to come along? Anyway. I'm going to bed soon, so don't call me tonight. Speak tomorrow."

She'd be working still. On shift until the early hours. I planned to be dead asleep by then.

* * *

But as it was I wasn't even in bed by then.

I was asleep on the sofa, the remains of a joint in an ashtray, finger still on the television remote where I'd been flicking through meaningless news channels.

My last thought before I crashed: *I'm in the clear... I'm a Dad.*

Chapter 36: Void

I dreamt of emptiness, blackness, a chasm swallowing me whole without even chewing. I dreamt of silence crushing my will, eager oblivion sucking the life from my tiniest movement.

This empty, searing void.

I dreamt and dreamt and could not, would not, wake up.

Even though I screamed into that silent vacuum.

Screamed.

And screamed.

I could not wake up.

I will not wake up.

*   *   *

I woke to the sound of my own screaming.

Lying contorted on the couch, where I had crashed after putting Bella down.

I hadn't had that dream for many years. Cold darkness as recurring nightmare; I must have been around thirteen. It came every night. That sense of silent, oppressive darkness, of sitting at the bottom of some unimaginably deep pit with nothing save the knowledge I was breathing; even that inaudible.

I always ended up screaming.

Screaming.

And unable to move.

Unable to move.

* * *

Like when he'd been behind me.

* * *

Like when I'd heard that Jamie was dead.

* * *

When I got back to the apartment my mother was waiting for me.

For once, there was emotion on her face, some tiny gleam in her eye.

I put down my stuff – I'd spent the day idling in Greenwich Village, watching the students from NYU, wishing that I'd studied enough to join them – not really caring, just wondering when I'd be able to get my next score.

It was still a few months before I'd see the gaping red smile of a bum's slashed throat.

I hadn't got the shakes just yet.

But they were coming.

I knew that.

"Kenneth," she said, framed in the living room doorway.

She was all flowing chiffon and expensive prints, choking scent and perfect hair. Disgust and harmony. Superiority and damnation.

My mother.

What is that look on her face? I thought.

"Yeah?" I answered, determined to retreat to my room, avoiding whatever it was she wanted to discuss.

I walked towards my room.

But it seemed that she was committed to the discussion. She moved to block my way, placing one hand on my chest. She didn't break eye contact and I couldn't avoid the gleam that shone there. She had steam pressure building up within.

"Kenneth."

"Yeah?"

"Will you stop for just one second," her lip actually curled into a smile as she continued, "I have something to tell you. Something important."

And just for a second, I thought that she might have had a sudden change of heart, be willing to undo the past twenty-odd years of my life, remorse and redemption, choosing to lay the peace-work of reconciliation. Some small, insignificant part of me wondered whether that was what was in her eyes.

For a brief moment, I was surprised to feel hope.

But it only lasted a second.

That bitch was as cold as the statues in Central Park.

Though at least they warmed up in the summer.

"Kenneth."

Like she'd only just learnt my name.

"Kenneth... Kenny..."

I stopped pushing against her hand. She had my attention.

"What?"

There was a moment of pause before she spoke and later, after I'd had chance to deal with what she shared, I would remember that pause. I would remember it forever.

Crystalline. Focused. Pure.

Her eyebrow raised slightly.

One corner of her mouth in that slight smile.

Her eyes grew even brighter.

There was almost a chuckle to her voice; a brook babbling over rounded pebbles.

"Jamie is dead," she said.

Then leant back to watch the show.

I was sure I hadn't heard her right.

"Jamie?" I asked.

She nodded, maintaining eye contact all the time.

"Yes," she said, just to make sure she was clear.

A punch to the gut. Winded; unable to breathe. Weight came down on me, pressing my shoulders, crushing my neck.

Jamie.

My mum.

My mother telling me my mum was dead.

"You gotta be kidding…"

She shook her head and I sensed her glee afresh.

"Huh… How?"

Jamie would have been in her late thirties at that time. Too young to have…

"How did she die?" my mother faked insouciance; butter wouldn't melt.

I nodded. Not really listening. Unable to hear anything past that ghastly look on her face; she was revelling in that moment.

My mother.

Bitch.

"Well," she began, "it seems to have ended up where it was always destined."

"Huh?"

"Oh don't tell me you didn't... No, of course not, you were only a child at the time. She was a junkie. Seems like she overdosed a couple of days ago. She died a junkie's death."

"No she wasn't, Ja..."

"Oh, not when she was on the show... Afterwards. Once it had all gone south. Look, Jamie was just a good time girl with great tits. The best she should have hoped for was a job in some little shoe shop somewhere. Give people like that money and they will always, *always* squander the opportunity."

I didn't catch much in the way of words as my mother spoke. All I was hearing was: *Jamie's dead, Jamie's dead, Jamie's dead...* But I did catch the tone in her voice, that resonance, redolent of the *Pimms and Lemonade* set that my mother had left behind in the UK. For women like her, the working class were nothing but butterflies on pins, to be studied, catalogued and filed under *'of passing interest'*. That and to provide service, obviously.

Tears pricked the back of my eyes, a lump forming in my throat. And a sudden pang that I wished I had scored and scored big that morning.

I wanted oblivion. I wanted emptiness.

I wanted to know what had happened.

"What happened?"

"As I said, an overdose," she stretched the *'s'* slightly, adding venom and irony. "Heroin. Seems like she had been in descent for a long time."

As I danced on the edge of understanding what I was being told, I was suddenly all too aware that I hadn't heard anything of Jamie for years and years. It must have been at least a decade. Back before puberty.

The last meaningful contact had been our last day on set. When the hugs had been reserved for everyone but the near-collapse kid in the corner, suffering from a depression that no child of five should ever have had to carry.

Jamie had sat with me for a while. Holding my hand. Talking about this and that. Talking about her plans. About how she was going to get into movies, where her real talent could show through. How when she made it, she'd look me up if any parts came through. And I stared into space. Not hearing. Not listening. Just staring.

The last time I saw Jamie, I didn't say goodbye.

"Yes, " my mother continued like she was telling someone about a soap opera she'd just watched on television, "it appears that Jamie didn't really do much after *Family Rules!* You know, the odd chat show, went on some celebrity quizzes, you know the sort of thing. Well, when the money dried up she…"

Another pause. And I knew she was using them on purpose.

"Well, she…"

"What?"

"She…"

Pause.

"According to Darren, she tried to get back in the newspapers but she was too old. They wouldn't have her."

Darren. Her golden boy paparazzi friend from London.

I could just hear his voice on the phone, telling her all this. The source of her glee.

"Once gravity goes to work, the pretty young things aren't nearly as alluring."

She barked a laugh. And I could have throttled her.

"Started out as just a nude scene in some cheap drama but within a couple of years, your friend Jamie was sucking cocks on VHS machines the country over."

Her eyes gleamed. She licked her lips like a wolf tasting blood, teeth bared in a snarl of pleasure.

"Of course, by this stage she was a regular junkie. A real mess. You should have seen the pictures. My Lord, she was a shadow of her former self."

She smiled at that.

And I suddenly read the jealousy in her, how much she must have hated Jamie becoming famous and adored, and I understood her sense of triumph at the news.

"Overdosed in an apartment in Amsterdam... I do hope she didn't suffer too much."

And there was so much sarcasm in that last sentence that it almost dripped on the carpet.

The bitch.

I pushed past her, trying to remember Jamie's face but finding it near impossible past the bile my mother had introduced.

I grabbed my bag and headed out of the apartment.

As the door was about to close, I heard her crow.

"Looks like we did the right thing getting you out of there!"

The door slammed behind me.

Chapter 37: Bubbles

I woke on the couch, as dawn's light spread through the apartment.

On my way to the bathroom, I glanced into the kitchen, where I found the light blinking on the answering machine. I stepped in, punched the button, waited for the pause, listened.

"Asshole."

Ivvy.

"I just got back in from the longest fucking evening and all you can do is leave me a message saying you're coming to stay with me? Is that it? After the past few days... What the fuck are you thinking? Asshole."

A click. She was gone.

I deleted the message on autopilot.

Walked through to the bathroom, eyes blurry with sleep and the hangover.

Left the door open as I took a leak.

"Hi!"

I jumped so high that I almost pissed on the cistern. Twisting to look over my shoulder, I found her standing there. Bella. My daughter. Smiling up at me. Wearing my mother's Nike work-out top, which nearly dragged on the floor around her feet.

"Just a minute," I said, quickly rearranging myself.

"Flush!" she commanded.

I complied, then turned to walk over to her; she pointed at the basin.

"Wash!"

I did a little double-take between her and the sink and then realised she was telling me to wash my hands.

Shit, I thought, *I'm being lectured by a two-year old kid.*

Dutifully, I walked over to the basin and ran the water.

From my side, she laughed.

"Bubbles!"

She was emphatic, and I presumed it was her way of telling me to use soap.

I made a great play of squeezing some of my mother's liquid soap from the dispenser onto my palms, rubbing up a lather. As I went to rinse, Bella held her hands out.

"What? You want to wash your hands?"

"Bubbles!" She smiled.

"Wash?"

She shook her head.

"Bubbles."

I looked in her blue eyes, her huge blue eyes, trying to work out just what she wanted.

She *must* have been wanting to wash her hands; the only logical conclusion. I looked around the bathroom. There was a small wooden stand with a neat stack of towels; Oliveria's touch again. I pulled it over in front of the basin and then held my hands out to Bella. She ran into them, laughing, and I transferred her to the wooden shelf.

"Thank you," she said, very prim, very proper.

"You're welcome," I smiled at the back of her head.

She grabbed hold of the soap dispenser and squeezed some into her palms; way too much, but she'd done it before I could think to caution her. She began to rub the soap all over her hands and then reached out towards the faucet. She looked up at me. Looked back at the faucet.

I turned the water on.

She rubbed her hands beneath the stream, getting a good, buoyant lather going.

I watched this with some good humour, this play act of washing, her dedication to turning her hands into massive mittens of bubbles. She was intent on her hands, paying me no attention whatsoever. I could have left the room and Bella would have carried on her *bubblicious* game.

But I was captivated, so I watched her from behind; in the mirror over the basin, I could just see her forehead, furrowed in concentration.

Then suddenly, she stopped rubbing her hands together. Held them in a prayer for a moment. Nodded. Linked her fingers together and pulled her thumbs down until there was a circle between them and her forefingers. She blew into the space and nothing happened.

A little grimace clouded her face for a moment.

She rubbed her hands together again and then reformed the shape. As she blew, more gently this time, a stream of small bubbles flew from her hands towards the mirror.

She squealed with delight.

"Bubbles!"

I couldn't help laughing.

She did it again. And again. And again. Each time that yelp of pure joy at seeing the bubbles race into the air.

She didn't try anything else and it became pretty clear that this was something she'd mastered, giving her so much pleasure that she wasn't about to stop. This was something she'd learned. Something she'd copied from...

Shit, I thought. Suddenly, I wasn't laughing; very near to tears.

Someone had taught her to do this. Her parents, a brother, sister, I didn't know, but it was someone who, until a little over a day earlier, had had a child, someone who at that moment was probably staring into an empty bedroom; a crib that hadn't been used for two nights.

Scattered toys and teddy bears; blankies left unloved.

"Bella," I spoke past the lump in my throat.

She looked up into the mirror, looked me straight in the eyes.

"Did your Mommy teach you to do that?"

She looked confused for a moment, like I'd spoken a language she had never heard before.

"Mommy?"

I nodded.

"Where Mommy?" she said, turning to look past me. As she did so, she lost her footing and tumbled off the towel stand, soapy hands flailing in front of her. She made to grab the edge of the sink but her hands were too slippery. She crashed to the floor of the bathroom.

Though I dived forward, I was too slow to catch her, ending up on my knees, staring at the tiles by the side of her head; the same tiles that my nose-bleed party-girl had covered with blood back when I was sixteen.

The flashback sight of the red spiders on the white floor was clear and clean but mercifully short.

Bella began to wail; screaming. Tears welled up in her eyes. In between screams, she wasn't breathing and each time she didn't inhale I thought she was about to pass out.

A bump the size of a small egg was beginning to form on her forehead.

I gathered her in my arms and began trying to calm her down.

It didn't work.

"Muh... Muh..."

"Take it easy, Bella, breathe," I spoke quietly; soothingly, despite the note of panic in my voice.

"Muh... Muh..."

"Shhhhh..."

"Mommy!" She screamed at the top of her lungs.

"Shhhhhh..."

"Mohhhhmmmmmyyyyy!"

"Mommy's not here, Bella," I whispered, fighting back tears that had constricted my throat, made my nose run, "Mommy's not here..."

Now my tears broke free.

We cried in the bathroom, me kneeling, Bella gathered in my arms, sobbing into my shirt, my own tears dripping onto the top of her head.

"Mommy's not here," I spoke into her hair, "I'm Kenny."

"I'm all you've got."

Chapter 38:
Ticker

While Bella sat at the table spooning milk-soaked cereal into her mouth – dropping most of it on the table, milk dripping down onto the expensive carpet – I watched CNN.

Stared into the space just in front of the television and thought about my parents. About Ivvy. About my little girl; my Bella.

Footage of war; exploded bodies, chaos in a market square, a car bomb in passionate pursuit of some cause, a child carried aloft, the final indignity of becoming symbolic effigy.

My eyes blurring with tears again.

Blurring.

```
       Child missing in New Jersey,
             mother dead
```

Cut to a talking head, some war correspondent or ex-General, explaining how it would all be so much easier if the US just got out of there and here was his three-step plan to remove the troops without leaving chaos in our wake. He nodded, smiled and frowned, emphasizing all the key points, as coached and air-brushed as any presidential candidate.

All for his thirty seconds of fame.

The anchor nodded as if he truly understood.

CNN. Vacuous at best.

Police hunt for father

The phone trilled.

"Phone!" Bella laughed from the table. The egg on her forehead had subsided somewhat, though it was already beginning to bruise.

I jumped to my feet, crossed the room and answered.

There was silence at the other end of the line.

Silence.

And I realized what I had just read on the ticker at the bottom of the screen.

Silence.

And I hoped it was another child they were talking about. Another child. Another mother.

Silence.

I looked at the back of Bella's head, tears flirting with my eyes.

"Hello?" my voice choking on the words.

"Great," Ivvy laughed out of the phone's earpiece, "that's all you've got? *Hello?*"

"Ivvy, I..."

I stared at the screen but the words had disappeared, scrolling off to reveal some stats relating to the war; body count and dead young soldiers, multiply by a factor of 100 to get the number of civilians;

piles of bodies rendered meaningless by repetition and objectification.

The talking head was still talking.

The anchor was still nodding.

Bella was still working her way through the cereal, dropping most of her breakfast on the table and floor.

Like a light switch, I made my decision.

The charade was in place. Like a war nobody wanted that had become a fixture of the daily news.

I was too far down the path to turn back now.

"… Thought you'd be sleeping?" I said.

"Couldn't," she said, "I had a long night and… Uh… It didn't go so well."

"What do you mean?"

"It… Oh nothing. You wouldn't understand. It's just… Just…"

```
Child missing in New Jersey,
mother dead
```

It scrolled across the screen again; a pointing finger.

"Are you OK?"

"Yeah. I'm fine. I just… Look, did you mean it that you and Bella are coming to stay here?"

The anger of her answering machine message was gone. There was almost a note of hope to her voice.

"Yes."

"That'll be good. What time do you think you'll be down here?"

"I don't know. Later today. Why?"

"Well, I need to clean up a bit and get some food. What does she like to eat?"

"At the moment? Cheerios."

"Very clever. I'll figure something out."

Police hunt for father

"I've got to go. See you later."

I put the phone down before she could respond, crossed to the television and turned up the volume. I sat on the floor, cross-legged, watching as the anchor turned to his second camera.

"Coming up after the break, a tragic story from New Jersey. A young mother taking her own life after her child is abducted. Police are hunting the father. More on this, and other developing stories, when we come back."

Chapter 39:
Being the Story

When I started reading the third page, he closed his eyes.

By the time I was on page four, he was nodding when I got to the end of a paragraph.

By the seventh page, it was rapture.

I looked up at him every so often over the top of the book. Careful not to move my head so I didn't break his trance.

I got to the end of the story.

And there was silence for a short while.

*   *   *

Finally, after what felt like minutes but was actually moments, his eyes flickered open.

His shining spectacles; reflected Manhattan skyline.

"Very good, Kenny," he said, "really. Very good."

I sat and said nothing, just stared at the table. My mind idled over the story; already forgetting bits of it. I took a drink from the glass of milk that sat by the book.

"You're quite the reader, young man. Quite the reader. Do you read a lot?"

I didn't say anything in response.

"Maybe with your parents?"

I shook my head.

"Really?"

"Uh-huh."

"Well, that seems a little odd. Your characterization, your pacing... I thought you must do a lot of reading."

I shook my head again, feeling the weight of the truth just behind my eyes.

Norris stared at me.

I had forgotten the story.

"They don't listen," I said, "they don't ever listen to me."

Sipped my milk.

Stared at the reflection in his spectacles.

*   *   *

Eventually, I flicked to the next story in the book and began reading.

And lost myself in images that got drawn between the words. I was the cowboy, I was the wizard, I was the caring mother, I was God. All of the *them*. All at once and whenever I walked on the page. I was all these things that I had never been.

Because if I hadn't, then I would have had to have been me. And I couldn't be me.

I couldn't.

There was too much beneath the surface of this pond.

Too much.

Too deep.

Dark things swam in the depths.

*　　*　　*

At the end of the story, Norris congratulated me again.

"Amazing," he said.

I had forgotten the story.

Staring into the abyss once more.

*　　*　　*

"Come on up," Ivvy said.

The door buzzed and I pushed it open.

"Come on, Bella," I said, reaching for her hand, "we're going to see Ivvy again."

"Ivvy?" Bella said and I couldn't remember whether I'd told her Ivvy's name earlier on. They'd certainly played together.

Do kids remember names, anyway? I thought.

We walked up the stairs. At the third flight, Bella stopped.

"I tired," she said, dropping the shopping bag she was carrying.

"It's only a couple of flights, c'mon," I smiled at her.

"Nooooo…" she wailed comically, "*I tired!*"

And she just sat down.

I was left there, standing at the top of the flight, weighed down with bags full of my clothes and the small amount of stuff I'd bought for Bella, two flights of stairs still to go and a recalcitrant toddler who refused to move another step.

I looked up, looked down, looked at Bella, looked back up the centre of the stairwell.

"Bella," I hissed but, if she heard me, she didn't acknowledge me in any way.

"Bella."

Still, no response.

I looked up, looked down, looked at Bella, looked back up the centre of the stairwell.

Caught in a loop.

Ensnared by the child.

I sat down next to her.

Getting angry. All of a sudden. Really angry.

```
            Child missing in New Jersey,
                  mother dead
```

And Bella wasn't moving.

"Come on, Bella, it's only a few more steps."

She shook her head.

"Tired."

I looked up, looked down, looked at the back of my eyelids while I tried to get some peace, some sense of calm enough to deal with the situation.

There'd been no other coverage on the news. Just that ticker along the bottom of the screen.

Had it been referring to Bella's mother or some other kid? I didn't know. They hadn't added any flesh to those skeletal words.

```
            Child missing in New Jersey,
                  mother dead
```

It had been enough to get me out of the apartment as quickly as I'd been able to pack.

And there I was, stuck on the stairs, two flights below the only person I could turn to, the only person with whom I had any form of relationship, any form of trust.

Ivvy.

My only friend.

Who happened to be a cop.

Police hunt for father

"Ivvy!" I yelled up the stairwell, *"Ivvy!"*

No sound, no response at the top of the stairs.

"IVVY!"

After a few moments, her head appeared over the banister, floating up there like a balloon.

"What?" she shouted down.

I looked up at her. Smiled as best I was able with the anger that was bubbling up inside me.

"Can you give me a hand?" I asked, "only Bella can't walk any more and I've got to carry all these bags."

Ivvy shook her head.

"What?"

"I can't."

My teeth were hurting where I'd clenched them together too hard.

My hair hurt, deep in the roots, my hair hurt.

"Why not?"

She leaned a little further out over the banister; topless.

"I was in the shower," she said, anger in her voice now.

"Oh."

"Yeah, fucking-oh," she was hissing again, almost snarling.

I glanced quickly at Bella to check whether she was listening but she was as non-cooperative as ever. If she'd heard Ivvy, there was no sign.

"Leave the bags down there and bring Bella up," Ivvy shouted, her head disappearing from sight, "I'll leave the door open."

And she was gone.

I put the bags to one side and then bent to scoop Bella up in my arms.

As I did so, she turned into my neck and snuggled tight.

And all of the tension flushed out of me.

She smelled good. Like soap. Like clean clothes.

I hugged her tight to me and just for that moment, in the dust motes and filtered sunlight of the stairwell, there was peace on Earth.

"C'mon, Bella" I whispered into her hair, "let's go see Ivvy."

I started up the stairs, Bella a half-ton weight in my arms.

"Ivvy," Bella laughed over my shoulder, "OK."

Chapter 40:
Click-Clack

Ivvy went to light a cigarette but then paused. Looked down at Bella.

"Bad idea, huh?"

I shrugged.

Bella was sat on the floor, playing with some beads. Ivvy had a whole random collection in a tin box, I had no idea why.

Ivvy put the cigarette down on the table with the lighter.

The beads *click-clacked* together as Bella dropped them in the tin.

"What am I going to do, Ivvy?"

She just looked at me.

And, to be honest, I hadn't known I was going to say that until I'd spoken.

"I can't see a way forward."

Or that.

"When are your parents coming back?"

"Tuesday. Tomorrow."

"What will they say when they know about Bella?"

Click-clack, click-clack.

"They can't know about Bella."

She snorted laughter.

The clicking stopped for a moment. Bella looked up at both of us with those almond eyes.

"She's a little hard to hide, Kenny. You can't stay here forever and, besides, surely this girl – her mother – is gonna come back looking for her some time?"

That phantom? I don't think so, Ivvy.

"They can't know."

Bella reached into the tin and pulled out a large, jade bead. She stared at it intently for a moment, a jeweller testing the cut of a diamond, and then held it up for us to look at.

"Lookit!" she exclaimed.

Ivvy looked at the bead, while I just glanced before re-launching my stare into space.

"That's pretty," Ivvy said, her voice developing a cadence I'd not heard from her before, "you like that one, huh?"

Bella nodded.

"Cool," Ivvy said and turned to look at me. "So how long were you thinking of staying here?"

I shrugged.

"Forever?"

I shrugged.

"Only you'd have to start paying some of the rent, you know? Get your name down on the resident's list and all that shit."

There was a tone coming into her voice. One that I *had* heard before; storm clouds threatened the horizon.

"Ivvy."

"No, come on… Isn't this just like you? You blow me off for days on end. With all that weird shit about the book and the photographs and then out of the blue, you're turning up here with your daughter who, by the way, you didn't even know you had until a couple of days ago, and telling me that you're staying here for you don't know how long but it's going to be more than a couple of days if your parents can't know about Bella, right?"

I knew what to do right then; I said nothing.

"Let's just say her mother doesn't turn up. That you're stuck with Bella forever. Are you planning to stay here with her until she's old enough to look after herself? There are girls on the street at thirteen. Are you gonna be around until she can make some money that way? Do you want her on her back at thirteen? Do you?"

There is no plan, Ivvy, I screamed inwardly, I haven't got one. I don't know what I'm going to do and I don't know where we're going to go.

I closed my eyes; found the ticker still running.

```
Child missing in New Jersey, mother
   dead — Police hunt for father
```

"What happened last night?" I asked, pure diversion.

"Huh?"

"Last night. You said on the phone that something happened."

Ivvy looked at me.

Click-clack.

"You could say that," she said, her hand toying with the lighter on the table.

Click-clack.

"I've been suspended."

I just looked at her.

Click-clack.

"Couple of weeks back, I did a deal with some undercover narc while I was working. Thought I knew everyone on the street. DEA got it and last night I got busted. Zero tolerance. Shit!"

She lit the cigarette then, hands shaking.

I hadn't noticed until now.

"Dope?"

She shook her head, a rueful smile ghosting her lips.

"They don't bust you for that. Just give you a slap on the wrist and ask you to pass the joint."

"Then what..."

"Smack."

She'd been clean for years.

"How could you?"

Now she raised an eyebrow, anger flooding into her.

"Oh sure! Now you're going to get all high and mighty on me... Well don't forget, mister *how-could-you*, that when I first met you, you were pretty much cold turkey. So don't go getting all judgemental on me... I don't need it. OK? I don't need it."

Click-clack.

A clock was ticking somewhere in the apartment.

Click-clack.

A siren blazed from the street below.

Bella played with the beads.

Click-clack.

Click-clack.

"Bella's not my daughter," I said before I knew I was going to say it, "I stole her."

"Fuck."

Click-clack.

Click-clack.

*   *   *

I laid it all out for her. Everything that had happened since the previous Friday night. Stealing the car, finding out Bella was in the back. The run across Central Park. My panic when Ivvy turned up. All of it.

The one thing I left out is the one thing she needed to hear; my decision that I would play the father. That Bella would be my daughter.

She knew only some of the emptiness between myself and my parents; the dark void of my nightmares.

"I think she was on CNN," I said, feeling tears beginning to prick my eyes, a lump beginning to form in my throat, "but I got jumpy and you'd phoned, so I figured I'd get out of the apartment sooner rather than later. And then…"

"Shhh, Kenny. Hush."

I fell silent. Watched her.

Click-clack.

She was thinking on something.

Stood. Crossed the room, turned on the small television on the kitchen counter, tuned it to CNN.

For five minutes we watched it without a word. Reading the ticker, watching the faceless anchor.

No mention of a baby missing in New Jersey, of a dead mother or absconded father.

We scanned other news channels. Nothing.

Ended up back at CNN.

The only other sound was Bella and her beads.

The lump didn't leave my throat.

After five minutes it was still fighting against my words.

"What am I going to do, Ivvy?"

She didn't respond for a moment. Just watched the screen. Waiting.

"Did you love her?" Ivvy said.

This stopped my thoughts dead. The lump disappeared.

"Huh?"

"Bella's mother," Ivvy wasn't looking at me, still staring at the screen, "did you love her?"

"Bella's mother was... I made her uh..."

"Truth, Kenny. Did you love her?"

I had no clue what she was asking me.

"What do you mean, Ivvy? I just told you all of it. Weren't you listening?"

I looked at her. Her profile. Her ratty blond hair, dirty with city grime.

"Are you still using?" I asked.

She didn't say anything for a moment or two.

"No," she answered, "but I was thinking about it last night. I've been on shift for the last week or so and... I don't know, I just got tired of it all. Tired."

She stared at the screen, lit another cigarette.

"Tired?"

"Yeah. The night-time, the marks, the girls. It never changes. And I'm tired of it."

"Don't they have... I don't know, like counselling or something? Like social workers?"

"Yeah, they've got that all right but this isn't stress or trauma or any of that shit. I'm just fucking tired."

Now, she turned to look me in the eye.

"So, just for a minute, Kenny. For a little moment or two, humour me. Let me have something approaching a normal conversation about normal things. About love and dating and sex and relationships. Talk to me like we're together, not just wasting time with each other. That's the conversation I want, Kenny. Normal. Not some act that I have to play every night."

Confused, I nodded.

"Good," she said. "Now, did you love her?"

"Who?"

"Bella's mother. Did you love her?"

Click-clack.

I saw type-written words on paper; dialogue and shooting directions. Dived into the abyss once more.

"For a moment," I said, "although on and off, we were together for a little over a year. It feels like I only really loved her for a moment."

"How did you know?"

"What, that I loved her?"

Ivvy nodded.

"I don't know. There was just a moment where I thought: *I love her, I really do*. But it was gone as soon as it arrived."

"Where were you?"

"Where?"

"Uh-huh."

"Where do you think?"

"Central Park?"

"No, guess again."

"Grand Central?"

Click-clack.

"Not even close. We were down at Chelsea Piers. It was raining and we were trying to get over the highway, over to the piers. It was really raining and I only had a light jacket; I was drenched head to foot. My trousers were too long, and they caught under my shoes as I walked. They were soaked through – all the way up my legs."

"Then, just for a moment, a gap came in the traffic and I grabbed her arm and we ran across the road. You know it's four lanes, so we dashed all the way, splashing and laughing and getting absolutely soaked."

"When we got to the other side, we were all out of breath but it was... What's the word? Exhilarating, I guess. Just so alive. And I looked at her, looked in her eyes and, just for that moment, it felt like I loved her."

My eyes snapped back to focus, my internal screenplay fading back into the mist.

Ivvy had tears in her eyes, welling on the lower lids.

"That's beautiful, Kenny," she said, "it must have been good for that moment."

I nodded; it had been. In my head, it had been.

"Can we keep her?" Ivvy asked, sounding so much like the kid who's persuaded a stray dog to follow her home that I did a double take, looking from Ivvy to Bella and back to Ivvy again.

Click-clack.

I shrugged.

"What do you think?"

"What do I think?"

I nodded the question again.

"I think we'd make great parents," she said, "that's what I think."

Neither of us said anything for a long, long time.

Click.

The anchor on CNN was the only one talking.

Clack.

We sat and stared at the space between us.

Click.

And considered what had just passed into that space.

Clack.

"Why not?" I said. And meant it.

"Yeah," Ivvy replied without a single pause, "why not?"

Chapter 41: Burst

An afternoon of CNN blurred our thoughts, turning us comatose with boredom. Switching to local news didn't do much else. Wherever we looked there was no mention of a child missing in New Jersey, mother dead or of a police force hunting the father.

A search on the web didn't find anything else.

"Do you think we should call CNN and ask?" I said at a little after four in the afternoon.

Ivvy just gave me one of her looks; raised eyebrow and turned-down mouth.

"No," I said, "bad idea. It's just… I mean…"

"Yeah."

I stared at the ceiling.

"Yeah."

* * *

"Let's eat."

It was early evening. We'd been stuck in all afternoon. I was hungry, claustrophobic and sick of television news.

Of bombed out buildings and food scares.

Of jet crashes and terrorism plots.

Of celebrity fuck-ups and their live-in fuck buddies.

My cremated brain cells.

"Chinese?" Ivvy shouted from the bedroom.

"OK," I replied, still staring at the screen. Grabbed the remote, brought blessed silence to the apartment.

Silence.

No over-stuffed talking heads spouting expertise for which no-one asked; for which everyone paid. No *coming up after the break*. No mention of a dead mother in Jersey or a father suspected of the killing. Nothing. Not a word.

Silence.

The non-sound of Ivvy moving around in the bedroom, getting changed. Cars and buses in the street below. The basso rumble of the subway thrumming deep beneath the building.

Silence.

A ticking clock in the kitchen area. Counting down the seconds. *Tick-tock*.

Tick-tock.

Ivvy was humming to herself.

And the rest of the apartment was silent.

Silent.

Tick-tock.

"*FUCK!*" I yelled.

There was no sign of Bella.

*   *   *

We scoured the apartment, finding nothing. It was Ivvy who got into the entranceway first and saw the door. It was open. Not ajar. Not on the latch. It was open.

"Shit," she breathed, "d'ya think..."

"I don't want to think," I said and headed out the door, "Bella!"

No response.

"Bella!"

No response.

I started down the stairs.

Knowing full well from the sound waiting to engulf me at the bottom that the door to the street was open. That Bella had walked out of the building into New York.

This wasn't yesterday in Central Park all over again.

This was much, much worse.

I started to take the stairs two-by-two, all the time shouting.

"Bella!"

When I got to the vestibule, my worst fears were confirmed. The door was open and Bella was nowhere to be seen.

I stepped out onto the sidewalk. Tried to put myself in the mind of a little kid. What would have attracted my attention?

An insane jumble of images, sounds and smells; confusion.

Ivvy caught up with me.

"Do you see her?" she spat out.

I shook my head. Looked up and down the street. Cars sped by, desperate to get through the stop-light before it turned. Taxis dissected the traffic like manic bumble-bees, diving and zipping here and there, gaining a yard wherever they could.

No Bella.

I looked at Ivvy.

"Did you leave the door off the latch?"

She looked at me.

"Did you?"

"I don't know," she said, "I can't remember. I might have done when I…"

And then we were quiet, each retracing the day in snapshots: of us arriving at Ivvy's building; of her being fresh from the shower; of her leaving the door open; of Bella and I walking up the stairs and…

"It was me," I said, "I left the door open when I brought the shopping up."

"Shit."

A taxi hit its horn loud enough to wake the dead.

Bella was somewhere out there.

*   *   *

We ran back up to the apartment, grabbed some cash, the keys.

I checked behind the couch, hoping that Bella had crawled there to grab some sleep. No such luck. I even looked in Ivvy's wardrobe.

We headed back downstairs.

Ivvy knocked at a door one flight down and an old woman answered.

"Hi, Eileen," Ivvy said to the old woman.

"Hi, sweetheart," Eileen responded, her initial smile at seeing her neighbour rapidly dissolving to concern, "are you OK?"

"I'm not sure," Ivvy said, "only my… our… Erm…"

"My daughter," I said, "she's gone missing."

Eileen was shocked.

"How old?"

How old is Bella? I thought.

"A little over two," I said, guessing.

"No way," Eileen gasped, "we should call the police."

"No," I said.

"No," Ivvy said.

Eileen just looked at us. I felt the flush rushing to my cheeks. Imagined that script again. Dialogue and direction. Dialogue and direction.

"She can't have gone far," I said, "she's just really tired and probably wandered down to the Deli. We'll just go and check."

Ivvy stepped onto the stage.

"Can you keep watch in case she comes back," she implored Eileen, "only we may miss her in the street."

"Could be she's up in your apartment and you just didn't spot her."

"Ivvy," I said feeling the pressure to be moving, "we need to…"

And Ivvy gave me a look I've only ever seen once before. In Soho when she played out her hooker double-life.

"You go, honey," she said, "I just want to clear things with Eileen. I'll meet you at the deli, OK?"

I'd just been given my orders.

"OK" I said and headed off down the stairs, leaving Ivvy to smooth things with Eileen and make sure there was no call to the cops. That all the old woman would do was watch the stairs for either our or Bella's return.

I emerged onto the street, desperate to find our daughter.

Taxis blared.

Garbage trucks crushed.

Pedestrians moved at speed without hitting each other.

A two-year old girl was lost in this.

Bella was lost.

Chapter 42:
Family Rules – Part XI

At age twelve, I read *Rogue Male*.

A year later, *Ring of Bright Water*.

Later that year, *The Woman in White*.

Filling my head with stories. With archetypes. With heroes, heroines and villains. With stories.

With avoidance.

*   *   *

A week after Norris suggested that I should pursue a career in the literary or dramatic arts, he was no longer my tutor, my parents exorcising him from my history as easily as they had England and my real, made-up family.

Every inch the Dickensian villains, they denied my pleasure, decreed my subjugation, forced my rebellion.

Shot in black and white, a script calling for sharp angles and incessant background noise. This melodrama they had created, with me the central character. Or was it victim? Who cared? Who really cared?

*   *   *

She was with her Upper East crones, debating fashion and what to do with the homeless multitudes that pestered one while one waited for a cab. When she got to talking about such subjects, with the right group of friends, she dropped straight into that accent, that *hoighty-toighty-might-have-known-the-Queen-herself*, upper class British bullshit accent; easy to imagine her the Queen of New York.

"Do you think Giuliani's going to do anything about them?"

She smiled coldly at the woman who had just spoken; her supposed best friend.

"That awful man. He's just awful. But he does seem to be speaking sense. There is all together too much crime in this city," my mother stated the obvious.

I sat outside the door, in the hallway of the apartment, staring at the other wall, thinking of Miss Haversham. Of Nancy.

Of *Rogue Male*, dug-in to his foxhole in the home counties, befriending a cat that ultimately provided the power for his sole weapon.

I sat in isolation; solitary confinement.

My mother and her friends clucked like chickens fresh from a cuckolding.

I felt like screaming.

It had been a month since Norris last came.

I ached for our lessons.

*   *   *

Thought of Jamie often.

Wondered what she would have been doing.

Would she still see Chris?

Was Chris still the good guy he'd always been?

Joel probably would have been pissing off another cast with his temper tantrums and angry crescendos.

Sanderson would be dead.

I hoped.

Jamie smiled in my dreams. I was old enough by then to know just what it had been that provided her allure.

I understood the titillation and flirtation. The ease with which she had carried herself. The woman beyond the breasts.

I understood why she'd been such a threat to anyone who held any notion of old-fashioned values.

Jamie came to me in my dreams.

And I welcomed her into my feverish, juvenile clutches.

She'd been the only woman I would ever love.

My mum.

Jamie.

*   *   *

My father looked at me.

He looked me up and down.

Slowly. Like he was reviewing a menu for a dish he'd never tried before.

The menu came up empty.

"Stop crying."

I tried, but I couldn't.

"I... I... I..."

Each word punctuated by huge, whooping breaths.

"Stop crying."

"I... I... I..."

He just frowned.

Scowled.

My father.

The bastard.

"Stop crying."

*   *   *

The script called for me to cry but by that time I was numb. I couldn't give anything. At five years' old, a husk.

I was about to enter the frame, Jamie and Chris running their dialogue on-set. Stung by a bee, I had to enter screaming; pretty much convinced that I was about to die.

I was arid.

"Start screaming before you come in, Kenny," Joel had said, "you really need to interrupt Chris when he's about to feed you the line.

The line.

"You bring the baps, I'm all about the sausage."

The inevitable grin to the camera.

Family Rules! had grown to cliché.

I'd nodded at Joel's direction. Nodding had become a good thing around Joel. A very good thing.

On-set, Chris delivered the start of the line.

"You bring…"

And Joel pinched me so hard on the leg that I screamed for real; immediate tears burning my eyes.

Awake for a moment.

I walked onto the set convinced that a bee had stung me.

Chapter 43:
Collapse and Retreat

I spent most of the afternoon moving around Ivvy's neighbourhood, dropping into shops, looking through windows, accosting people with a simple question.

"Have you seen a little girl?"

Repetitively. Always the same answer.

I moved from sprinting to running to speed-walking until, by the time an hour of searching had gone I was walking, no longer even annoyed by the people who got in my way.

And all the time a thought had been growing.

It didn't matter.

I only fought it back for about twenty minutes, and wasn't that surprised to find it growing. I hadn't asked for this child to come into my life.

I had *not* asked for this child to come into my life.

Once I'd taken down the barricades, the thought put on weight; a burgeoning thunderhead.

At one point, I'd caught a glimpse of a child down the street, between wandering adults, and I rushed forward. It had been a boy.

I'd looked in the other direction, tried to remember if I'd been down there?

And thought: *why should I?*

A deli on the corner... Though I'd been in there earlier on, I considered whether I should loop back once more.

Once again: *why should I?*

And on.

And on.

* * *

Ivvy and I wound up bumping into each other a couple of blocks away from her apartment. She had a wild-eyed look, sweat streaming down her face. Breathing heavy.

"I've..." she panted, "covered the... whole... of... of..."

And couldn't go on. She breathed. In and out.

I scanned up and down the street and quickly realised that I wasn't looking for Bella. I was assessing whether anyone was actually watching this conversation.

Already covering my tracks.

I thought of a gaping wound across the throat of a bum.

Stealing clothes from someone who has none.

"I haven't seen her," I said and had a moment to wonder at how blank my voice sounded.

"Where did you look?" Ivvy said, her breathing coming back under control.

I shrugged.

"Places."

She looked at me askance, raising an eyebrow.

"Places?"

"Yeah. Places."

She said nothing in response.

I scanned the street again.

"How old is she, do you think?" Ivvy asked.

There was a guy on the corner, grooving to the sound of his iPod; trademark white ear buds, as much a tribal statement as a tattoo. The street-corner, the moment, was his and his alone.

"Huh?"

I tried to guess the song from the rhythm of his groove.

"Kenny?"

I nodded in time with his head.

"Don't do this, Kenny."

Nodding.

"She's just a kid! Don't do this. Don't you…"

I walked past Ivvy, heading down the street, towards the guy but meaning to go past him. My steps fell to the rhythm of his head. I got a couple of steps and then she punched me on the shoulder.

"Kenny! You fuck!"

I kept walking.

The city noise blurred into a cloud and I moved through it and in it, at the same time stepping aside to a place where I couldn't even observe myself. The only sensation my feet hitting the pavement and the rhythm of that guy's head.

I hadn't asked for this child to come into my life.

Today was no different than four days earlier.

No different.

The kid had been a mistake. An accident.

"Kenny!" Ivvy gave a last desperate cry. "What about Bella?"

My voice was little more than a whisper in response. It seemed to me that it came from far, far away.

"You want her? You can keep her."

I floated past the guy on the corner and didn't even turn my head to look at him. What Ivvy did next, I didn't know. And, at that moment, I didn't really care.

The sensory avalanche of New York enveloped me.

The script had called for the end credits.

I was no-one and nobody again.

Retreating.

Chapter 44:
The Camera Pans Away

I was heading toward the subway, still nodding to an imagined groove; grey fog enveloped memories of Bella's face, Ivvy's desperation. Nodding. Nodding.

Fog.

Stepping-in-time to an imagined drummer.

The first hand grabbed my right shoulder from behind, the second my left wrist, twisting my arm up between my shoulder blades and it felt like my shoulder was about to dislocate. Turned me sideways, slammed me against the window of an electronics shop, nose but a few inches from electric razors, cheap digital cameras and tiny statuettes of liberty.

I couldn't see who was attacking me, but before I could do anything something hard was pressing against the back of my neck; a billy club? Kicks to the inside of my ankles, spreading my legs.

"You," a voice charged with adrenalin and the chase, "have the right…"

I listened to the rest and waited until they dragged me into the car or truck or whatever other vehicle they were going to use to take me in.

*   *   *

As they walked me from the truck into the precinct, I saw her watching from a discrete distance.

The talented actress.

Whose panic and care now looked like so much cheap make-up.

*   *   *

Stared at the camera.

Hugh Grant.

Bobby Brown.

Glen Campbell.

Nick Nolte.

Tupac Shakur.

Me.

Stared at the camera.

Staring at the camera.

Staring into the camera.

Staring...

*   *   *

The camera is a deep black hole and, for the first time in a long time, it has sucked him down into its deep, abiding vortex.

He stares and stares, spent from the telling; cathartic husk.

The audience silent.

The gleaming, monochromatic eye reflecting his distorted face.

Absolution.

Penance.

Lost in it's dark, circular logic.

"We're here with Ken Walsh who has been sharing the true story of what happened last summer," the host smiles at the camera, "more when we come back from this break."

The red light on the camera shuts off.

*   *   *

One of the writers steps up onto the set, crosses to the host, and kneels by her side.

"You OK?" he asks.

"Uh-huh."

"Only..."

"What?"

"Well... er..."

"You didn't expect this?" Kenny speaks slowly and quietly, fighting hard to retrieve his focus from the dark centre of the dormant camera lens.

They both turn to look at him. Shake their heads in agreement.

Kenny smiles sadly.

"I wish I had," he said, "only it'd be a lie. I've... Often wondered what it would be like to tell it all. To come clean. And I thought about it a lot while... While I was away. But I never thought..."

"One minute!"

The host and writer flinch a little at the floor manager's time call. Kenny doesn't register any reaction; too great his conditioning at the hands of Joel's mercurial temper.

When Kenny turns to look at them, he sees that the host is close to tears, watching him as a mother would a wounded infant, all succour and sympathy, a hug not far behind.

"What?" he asks.

A tear breaks loose and she catches it with the tip of her index finger.

Before it can hit her make-up, naturally.

She hasn't become the most famous woman on television without becoming the consummate professional.

"Twenty seconds!"

The writer leaves the stage.

She doesn't respond to Kenny's question, just showers him with that maternal gaze of love.

"Ten! Quiet on set!"

The countdown begins.

Familiar theme music sounds across the studio, familiar lights coming up on familiar stage set, familiar couches.

No tears for our host now.

"Welcome back. We're here with Ken Walsh, who you'll know as Walter from *Family Rules!*, the UK comedy currently airing on Nostalgia TV's *'Back To The 80s'* channel. We've been hearing about his role in the abduction and loss of a small child in New York city last year. Jeannie Jameson is here to remind us of the story."

Cut to the pre-recorded loop. Two minutes of facts. The stolen car, the child, the lost weekend, the loss and subsequent hunt.

Three days he had sat in that cell, waiting to hear something, anything, about Bella. When they'd finally told him, it had been as an afterthought. He hadn't realised until that moment how much he had expected to hear the worst.

The loop ends, cut back to the host.

She looks at the camera.

"An amazing turn of events, I'm sure you agree," she says and then turns to face him.

"Ken," she says, "you must have thought long and hard whether to tell us everything you have tonight?"

She is consummate.

"What was it like, stuck in that cell and not knowing whether Bella was alive or dead?"

He nods, catching the gleam in her eye – the comfort of safety in this place, her cathedral – turns to face the camera, stares into the dark circle.

"It's hard to explain," he says, "there were nights when I really could have ended it."

Camera cuts to the wince on the host's face.

"But I was... Waiting, I guess. Waiting for something. Confirmation either way."

She nods.

He thinks of the few, empty conversations that he has shared with his parents over the past year; familiar vacuum.

"That weekend... For that weekend," he flicks his head towards the overhead monitors to indicate the video loop, "I loved Bella – she was my daughter and I *was* her father."

Slight gasp in the audience. Not used to such candour, such transparency.

"And even though I'd been telling myself I didn't care, the truth is I did."

"So when they came to you and told you that Bella..."

"Yes... That was so hard. So, so hard."

Tears are welling once more in the host's eyes.

Kenny tries to speak a couple of times but his throat has closed; when his voice emerges, it is tiny.

"Thank God she's all right."

"Amen," the host says.

Fade from tears on a television host's cheeks to pictures of a little three year-old running around, playing with her mother. This smiling infant, innocent in play and already oblivious of her lost weekend in New York. Of blowing bubbles from the sink, of seeing her would-be father rescue her in Central Park, of being carried through Strawberry Fields late at night. Oblivious in play with her mother.

Throughout the video, shown to audience, cast and crew on overhead monitors, Kenny keeps his eyes firmly closed, humming slightly to tune out the sound of Bella's laughter.

On the screen, his daughter.

Behind his eyelids, the depth of the camera's lens.

On his lips, the theme tune for a make-believe family far, far behind in the rear-view mirror.

Empty, Kenny awaits his next cue.

Also available by
Vincent Tuckwood

"Escalation"
A Novel
Vincent Tuckwood

Shocked by the violent beating of their popular high-school quarterback, a small New England town immediately calls for justice, and for police chief Jack Baker to restore order.

Caught in the political spiral of the town elders and their ten-cent dictator, first selectman Mason, Baker has no choice but to place one of his most trusted officers, Charlene Goodlow, in the school.

As Baker manages the *'grown-ups'* of the town, Charlene soon finds that she is regressing, her own long-buried high school anxieties returning to gnaw at her.

Increasingly isolated and frightened, Charlene finds herself at the corner of a vicious triangle of lust and animosity; as the violence and tension escalate, she slips further down the rabbit-hole, until she is left with a teenage boy in the sights of her police issue revolver and the singular decision of whether or not she will pull the trigger.

'Escalation' is a fast-paced work of contemporary fiction, deeply rooted in the darkest of unintended consequences.

"Karaoke Criminals"
A Novel
Vincent Tuckwood

In *Music, Musica*, a karaoke bar on the Spanish riviera, Roxi is about to discover that her dreams may come true when Brian Ferguson offers to hook her up with his connections back in London. Roxi has no idea of the price attached to this offer; Brian doesn't do anything without good reason.

And for Miles Ashley, who thought he'd escaped Brian's clutches years earlier, a single phone call is enough to stop the song, rewinding the tape to zero.

Throw in an A&R rep under threat of castration and an exquisitely dangerous hood on the verge of a nervous breakdown and it's time to make music; gunfire drumbeats, filter sweep of cordite.

As the double-crosses, gang wars, reclaimed favours and challenged loyalties intertwine, it's clear that only blood spilled in revenge can clean the slate ready for Roxi's success.

In this part of the world, this is how business gets done.

Even the music business.

'Karaoke Criminals' is a fast-paced contemporary novel, the bastard offspring of *'The Commitments'* and *'Lock, Stock and Two Smoking Barrels'*. Music has never been this dangerous.

"Do Sparrows Eat Butterflies?"
A Novel
Vincent Tuckwood

In a moving tale of one man's search for meaning in an increasingly lonely and depressing life, a washed up seaside painter embarks on a journey that will change him forever.

Bored, lacking inspiration and verging on alcoholism, Ray encounters a man burning alive as he walks the beach near his home. The painter is persuaded to visit the burnt man's home, Certainty, where a commune gathers under the spell of its enigmatic leader, Ged. Although it seems the idyllic embodiment of counter-culture freedom, Ray discovers that Certainty is far from ideal. Something insidious, something evil, lurks just beneath the surface.

As his unusual, traumatic rebirth unfolds, Ray discovers the horror of an inferno he has denied for years. To save the love that can provide true meaning in his life, he has no choice but to answer that one, repeating question: *do sparrows eat butterflies?*

'Do Sparrows Eat Butterflies?' is a deeply absorbing story of redemption, acceptance and love. A journey into the shackled heart and soul of an artist, it will leave you profoundly changed.

"Garbled Glittering Glamours"
Words from 2010
Vincent Tuckwood

I yearn only for now

Reminisce
Remember
Love your memory
Accept the you that was
Yet know
your now will become
your was
Is your is
all the was
you'd have it become?

'Garbled Glittering Glamours' is a collection of poetry published at
VinceT.net and elsewhere in 2010.

Boutique Empire is an artists' collective, proudly centred around the Vancouver, Canada music scene, Boutique Empire is currently home to: Sex With Strangers, Combine The Victorious, Guilty About Girls, Gilles Zolty, the graphic art of Robert Edmonds, the fashion of Isabelle Dunlop, and the stories of Vincent Tuckwood.

Vincent Tuckwood is a story-teller working in fiction, song and verse. At any given point in time, he's proud to be a father, husband, son, brother, cousin and friend to the people who mean the world to him.

He is the author of the novels *"Escalation"*, *"Family Rules"*, *"Karaoke Criminals"* and *"Do Sparrows Eat Butterflies?"*, as well as the 2010 poetry collection, *"Garbled Glittering Glamours"*. His screenplays are *"Team Building"*, and the screen adaptation of Family Rules, *"Inventing Kenny"*.

Vince regularly connects with his audience at VinceT.net and at his story-teller page on Facebook, often writing poetry in response to their prompts, and encourages everyone to get in touch there.

Made in the USA
Charleston, SC
17 December 2011